Copyright © 2023 by Scott J. Moses
Cover Art © 2023 by George Cotronis
First published in 2023 by DarkLit Press

ISBN 978-1-7386585-8-9 (Hardcover)
ISBN 978-1-7386585-7-2 (Ebook)

PRAISE FOR
OUR OWN UNIQUE AFFLICTION

"Unexpected and grim, Scott J. Moses' *Our Own Unique Affliction* is the most inventive and bombastically gruesome vampire story I've read since *The Light at the End* by John Skipp and Craig Spector. An exquisitely written meditation on grief, family, and trauma told with such empathy and care. I feel broken after reading this book, and I applaud Scott for obliterating my soul with such grace and tenderness."

- Eric LaRocca, author of *Things Have Gotten Worse Since We Last Spoke and Other Misfortunes*

"Scott Moses writes from a place of pure empathy, the result of which is a story that pulls the reader in with deceptive ease, putting them through the emotional wringer, culling fear from every page. A tightly written fever dream of bloodlust and family ties, grief, rage and the eternal hunt."

- Laurel Hightower, author of *Crossroads* and *Below*

"Weaving elements of family, grief, and eternity, Moses' *Our Own Unique Affliction* explores the familiar, in not so familiar ways, in a hypnotic and terrifying tale."
- Cynthia Pelayo, Bram Stoker Award Nominated author of *Children of Chicago*

"Moses gives us not only complicated and relatable characters, but also cinematic scene-setting coated with pathos and grit. *Our Own Unique Affliction* forces readers to face that often circumstance is the only thing separating us from the monsters."
- J.A.W. McCarthy, Shirley Jackson Award nominated author of *Sometime We're Cruel and Other Stories*

"Moses tenders a vampire's origin and fate in the skin of a mood-soaked tragedy, embraced by bloody nights and unyielding regrets. Fans of Paul Tremblay's *The Pallbearers Club* should sink their fangs in before sunrise."
- Hailey Piper, Bram Stoker Award-winning author of *Queen of Teeth*

"An interesting psychological twist on the vampire narrative. Definitely a fun read."
- Charlene Elsby, author of *Hexis, Psychros, Menis*

BOOKS BY
SCOTT J. MOSES

Hunger Pangs

Non-Practicing Cultist

What One Wouldn't Do

OUR OWN
UNIQUE
AFFLICTION

SCOTT J. MOSES

DarkLit
PRESS

CONTENT WARNING

The story that follows may contain
graphic violence and gore.

Please go to the very back of the book
for more detailed content warnings.

Beware of spoilers.

For Shmuel Fischler,
without whom this book wouldn't be possible.
Thank you for helping me enjoy "what if" again.

And for Kelly Berry, if there is light, I hope it
found you.

"Blood has been harder
to dam back than water."
—Robert Frost, "The Flood"

"You should remember
that you were born to die."
—Curley Weaver and Blind Willie McTell,
"You Was Born to Die"

CONTENTS

CHAPTER 1
HUNGER PANGS

Night smothers the city as rain glides down the shoulders of my scuffed leather jacket. A gift from someone who won't need it anymore. I sniff the air, gaze shifting to the stale dumpster in the rear of the alley. A rat stands upright, head at a tilt. It hisses and scurries off. I fight the urge to hiss back.

My phone buzzes in my pocket. Probably Hannah Grace, tapping her foot by the big rig, checking her phone every five minutes like some overbearing mother. I take it most older siblings are like that, when no mother figure is around.

I flip open the phone.

Hannah Grace: Bodachi doesn't want to wait any longer. We've a long road to Boston and it's near midnight. Dine, don't make a scene, and get back here. Early bird gets the worm, Alice Ann.

—What if the worm sleeps in?

Hannah Grace: ...

I close the phone with a sigh.

When will she realize we're no longer slaves to time? What are we but nonchalant shadows in a world overrun with hurry?

My phone lights up, buzzes in my hand.

Hannah Grace: You okay? You've been off lately…

I stare at the text, thumbs hovering over the keys. I'd hold my breath if I had breath to hold, so instead I flip the phone shut.

My boots splash puddles as I make for downtown. The skyline blossoming with electric light in the night. I smile at the slow-burning embers in this sea of steel and concrete. The city's vibrance insulting the natural order, just like me. The cars parked along the street never cease to amaze me. How the molds surrounding familiar logos shift and reaffirm themselves. Like us, in a world that's changed so much in the last two hundred years. This world is new; it never sleeps.

I hear them before I see them, a line of them, standing in their Sunday best to do the devil's work. A brute in a pinstripe suit, clipboard in hand, looms over the entrance to the chaos within. The deep pulse of the thumping bass reverberates from within the three-story club. White brick walls accented in broad black slants spiral down to the pavement, an attempt to be hip. Do humans say *hip* anymore?

I fall in line behind a pair of girls, blonde and brunette, wearing short dresses that cling to the curves of their haunches. The whirring headlights of passing traffic whiz by, kicking up mist when a car veers close to the curb.

"I can't wait to get inside," the brunette says, her fingers stretching the fabric of her dress over her thighs. "It's so *cold* out here."

The teeth *above* my teeth quiver, and my tongue glides over them as they descend in anticipation.

Pairs are harder, but more rewarding.

The blonde reaches into her hardly-qualifying-as-a-bag and removes an orange prescription bottle.

"Here, babe," she says, plucking a pill from the container, extending it to the brunette with painted nails. "This will warm you up."

"Sarah!" The brunette says, head whipping around as she recoils from the drug. "With all these people, are you *insane*?"

They laugh and slide the pills beneath their tongues. I doubt they know they've saved themselves. Blood tastes different when the host is under the influence. Alcohol is rampant, so you get used to it, but anything more tastes foul.

Their eyes meet mine.

"Want some, honey?" the blonde says, giggling, blue irises surrounding pinpoint pupils.

The drug taking effect.

She extends the bottle, the brunette smirks beside her.

I check my burner.

11:25 p.m.

3 | SCOTT J. MOSES

Flipping it shut, I look her in the eye, my gaze an invitation she can't resist.

Hook.

Traffic stills as I home in on her, and her breathing slows.

Line.

Her pupils enlarge.

Sinker.

"Are you sure you want to let me ahead of you? I mean, you've been waiting so long."

Her mouth falls limp, eyes fully dilated now. She says, "Of course, yeah…go ahead."

"Sarah, what the hell? We've been freezing here an hour." The brunette glares at me. "Look bitch, we—"

Her mouth melts with my gaze, pupils dilating like the blonde's.

I smile, say, "Walk into the street."

She trembles, straightens. "Oh…sure, sure…"

She steps to the curb, clutching her bag, the red-yellow lines of downtown traffic in bloom.

Hannah Grace's words echo in my mind.

Don't make a scene…

I take her wrist, she jolts.

"It's fine," I tell her. "Thanks for letting me ahead of you."

I nudge by them, continuing the *Simon Says*

dance. Manipulating my way through the hoard of suits, dresses, and flamboyant scents these humans lather themselves in, my nostrils burning.

"What do you mean you're *at capacity*?" a young man in a sports jacket says, hair-gel dripping to his collar, hands on his hips.

The bouncer, a tall dark glass of *seriously, don't fuck with me*, towers a full head over the man, or rather, boy.

"I mean what I mean," the bouncer says. The boy rears to say something else, but the giant points to the street.

"Beat it."

The boy does so.

The giant glances at his clipboard and then to me. He sighs, and I know why.

I look young, about two weeks into twenty-one. So being carded is *in the cards* for me until the sun explodes or the drinking age is lowered. My money's on the sun.

"I'm gonna need some ID, miss." His eyes graze mine, too quick to capture.

I hand him a crumpled coupon from the inner pocket of my leather jacket.

"Ma'am, this isn't—"

"I was raised by two left-handed hags."

He looks at me, brow raised, and his expression goes slack, pupils dilating like those of the girls before. He's no moron though, and his mind pulls away. My eyes widen, and it's then the mental hooks extend, burrowing deep into his psyche.

"How, old…are you...?"

"Old enough, big guy. You're a credit to your species."

"Okay…enjoy your evening." He extends the coupon back to me.

"Keep it," I say, and he nods, opening the metallic door. I pass through, fingertips massaging my throbbing temples. Once you have their eyes, they're malleable, susceptible to influence.

The bass rattles my bones. The room is dark, though I can't remember *true* dark. Piles of people sway to the music, stamping their feet, grinding beneath the rays of green and yellow strobe lights. There's a sexual energy here, and the air swells with alcohol and sweat.

My mind wanders to the jazz clubs of the 1930s, now *that* was music. Not this *"march to the beat, everything's all right"* white noise. But hey, can't have everything now, can you?

I shoulder my way through the sheep and lean on the bar, which doubles as an island in the center of the club. The hole of the donut. I smile at the barman, a thin man with his hair buzzed at his temples and wearing a suit vest. I order a whiskey. A spherical ice cube bobs in the amber poison, and I slide the barman a ten-dollar bill. Some professions garner a kind of *default* respect with me, and bartender is one of them.

On stage, a pair thrust their fists upward and the crowd does the same. The music stops. The lights die. The masses cheer in the silence. The beat drops again. Spotlights float along the crowd in a strobe of renewed chaos. The bar trembles with electronic music, and the manufactured sound travels through the soles of my boots.

I check my phone.

11:40 p.m.
Hannah Grace: Update?
—Looking over the menu.
Hannah Grace: It's not a sit down kinda night, more drive-thru. Bodachi's on my ass.
—Won't be long.
Hannah Grace: Uh huh…

Bodachi will give me hell if I'm not back soon, and for good reason. He doesn't have an affinity for sitting still given his *cargo*. Given, what we are. I give humans a lot of shit, but alongside the barman, Bodachi has my utmost respect. Few of us have the luxury of traveling in daylight, and it's people like Bodachi who make it happen for us. Make it so my sister and I aren't confined to the sewers or metros of some lone city. We get to explore, and Bodachi is our conductor, our family. Despite his mortality.

I close the phone and bring the whiskey to my

lips. Bodachi says whiskey burns because it's cleansing the soul of wretchedness. I try to imagine how that feels, a redemptive flame wiping away all misdeeds, mistakes…malformations, like me.

I'm elsewhere.

Far from the relentless booming of the digitized bass.

Hannah Grace and I in the field of dandelions outside our farmhouse.

Ma tends the garden, and Pa plows the fields with an ancient donkey whose name I can't remember. I hear them speaking, and though I can't make out the words, I smile.

The wind and sun on my face.

Warmth.

Light.

Hannah Grace looks to me, smiling as well. The definition of safety. Contentedness.

It's funny really, how what was comfortable can turn on you. Can become the very thing capable of killing you in a world where you're all but untouchable.

The ice shifts in my whiskey, and my eyes glide over the ocean-esque mass of human beings. A body of alcohol-laden water, its surface a thousand swaying hands shining *purple-white-green* in accordance with the heartbeat of the bass.

Pulse-pulse.

A quintet of university boys, raising shots at the bar. All smiles, collars popped.

Pulse-pulse.

A triangle of girls, sipping on done-up drinks of purple and blue, hands and glasses pulled inward, swaying to the music.

Pulse-pulse.

I close my eyes, lost in the mingle of heartbeats.

Pulse-pulse.

Sweat.

Pulse-pulse.

Heavy breathing.

Pulse-prey.

Prey-prey.

Preypreypreypreypreypreypre—

Saliva lines the corners of my lips.

Composure, Alice Ann. Composure.

The music rises, and I scan the sea for stragglers, for the sick calves wandering too far from the others.

A girl wearing male genitalia as a hat. The ribbon across her white dress reads: *Bride to Be.*

A man, lifted by two others, suit covered in vomit, holds his hand out to one of the bouncers, a rhinoceros of a man, who's pointing at the door.

Sick, yes. Alone, no.

My stomach growls and I lean forward. My fangs lowering with the barman's approach.

Shit.

"Fine over here, doll?"

"I'm good."

"Well, let me know if—"

I don't hear the rest.

On the outskirts of the crowd, a couple are in disagreement. Her head is in her hands, and when he places his own on her shoulder, she knocks it aside. He looks to the musicians on stage, begins nodding with the music. Head shifting to the woman, who's weeping in her hands. I sip my whiskey, taking in the nightlife theater.

The man points to the bar, says something, and when she looks up at him, he goes in for a kiss. She knocks him away, arms flailing. I can't read her lips, but she spits flame before walking off. My eyes follow her as she flashes her neon bracelet to the bouncer standing at a door bathed in green, then yellow, then green. He opens the door, and she passes through.

I smile.

The man sits at the bar opposite me. His brown hair tussled and laden with sweat, eyes bloodshot, drunk. His collar is ruffled, the hint of spilled alcohol running down his shirt. Breathing heavily. Neon bracelet on his wrist.

I run a hand through my hair, settle my stone-set gaze on him. He's drumming his fingers on the bar, stops when he notices me. My eyes pull him in a moment, and then leave him stranded, chin in his hands. Stupid look on his stupid face. I don't need him slipping into a trance across the bar and getting wheeled out on a stretcher. He circles the bar, and the old part of me, the naïve part, wonders if he'll mind that I smell like the wooden pallets and plastic wrap of Bodachi's big rig, but the thought dies with the remembrance that *I am new, I am dead, and I am alive. I am, and I am not.*

He sits next to me and waves over a confused bartender, who holds a shot in each hand.

"So," he begins, glancing to where he and the woman once were. "I got these for someone else, but that's not going so well."

My stomach groans, and I feel his eyes all over me. My nails dig into the granite bar, fangs clenched.

He reeks of vodka.

I turn away, sip my whiskey.

His hand finds the small of my back, and my teeth clench, fangs bared.

"What do you say? Wanna—"

I turn to him, finding his eyes. "Your bracelet. What's it for?"

He's drooling, though I'm not sure whether it's from libido, hypnosis, or both.

"V.I.P....re-entry...meet DJs after—"

"Give it to me."

He slides it off, extends it my way.

I down the whiskey and rise to my feet.

"Why don't you have those shots yourself?" I say, sliding my empty glass to the inner side of the bar. "And a double shot of whiskey every ten minutes until the barman refuses to serve you."

"All...all right," he says, or rather moans. I wave down the barman and slide him a one-hundred-dollar bill.

"Whatever he wants," I say, nodding to the

man downing back-to-back shots. "He's my brother, and I'm his ride home. He thinks he can out-drink me, but I'm ex-military, baby."

The barman laughs, and I wink, making my way to the metallic door beaming—*yellow green yellow green.*

The rhinoceros bouncer, formidable beard making up for the shine of his shaved head, stares down at me. He points to a neon bracelet on his wrist, his expression stone. I flash my own and curl a finger toward him. He bends low and I stare into his pale blues, watching his pupils grow. I bring my mouth to his neck, just below the ear, fists clenched to restrain myself from draining him then and there.

"No one in or out of this door unless they're with me."

I step away, and he's nodding. Mouth hanging open like some thirsty dog.

The door wrenches open with a squeal.

Mist swells in the alley when my boots hit the glistening pavement. I lift my nose to trace her scent, stop at the *click-click-clicking* of nearby heels. She's pacing, phone to her ear. Her other hand wiping tears from her face, mascara running in lines.

"I know, Mom. It's hard, but I'm fine."

Her fingers comb through her brown hair,

lifting and letting it fall as she's blinded by tears.

"I know, I love you too...I'm fine, really." She lowers the phone and the screen fades to black. She stumbles, arms outstretched, clearly drunk, and slumps down to the curb. The iPhone *click-clacking* on the cement beneath her.

I glance at the rooftop above us.

Dinner with a view.

I'm a few feet away when she looks up at me, tears filling her eyes. And yet, she's calm, as if expecting someone all along. She chuckles, sighs.

"You know those ads on social media? The really click-baity ones?"

I gauge the weight of the rusted fire escape protruding from the bricks above us, wondering if it will manage our combined weight.

My eyes find hers a moment, but she breaks away. Seems the iPhone is the superior hypnotist here.

"Kendall pumps her own gas and more ways celebs are just like us!" she says, arms in stilted movement, like some animatronic mascot at some touristy carnival. "It's bullshit, all of it...like, how you can lie to your family when they ask if you're okay. Like, what I'm doing tonight, at some club I can't even stand..."

You okay? You've been off lately...

I lower myself to the curb beside her.
The hell am I doing?

"And what is that exactly? What you're up to tonight."

Her chin slips from her hand before she speaks.

"Oh, you know, randomly messaged one of my *matches* for a drink. No strings, just booze and a quick lay, to not think for a goddamn second."

I resist asking what a *match* is. Humans of today are strange.

The bluest moon looms over us, and my stomach wrenches. "Thinking is like life, some insatiable hunger you'll never quite satisfy."

She chuckles, runs a hand through her hair. The neon wristband catching in her brunette-locks.

"My brother preached something similar, that nothing matters. And you know what? He killed himself a year ago tonight, but for someone who thinks nothing matters, well, that's the only logical choice, right?"

"I'm sorry for your loss."

"I've had a hell of a year without him. My studies are slipping, I'm late more and more to my job. I don't know, it's just, if nothing matters, if nothing *really* matters, then being alive is the biggest loophole in the universe and we should take advantage of it. That's what I should've told him, what I would've told him if he'd called that night. He sat alone in his apartment, feeling that regardless of nothing mattering he was a failure. That he'd let everyone down. Why leave a note at all, Michael, if nothing matters?"

That word…*alive*.

Of a life once had, in the sunlight. Something beyond sleeping between stacks of pallets and animal feed. Something beyond driving cross-country with a sister I've known two lifetimes but can't talk to about these *longings*. Of wanting to feel the sun, hell, even see it just one more time, fully aware of the consequences. A warm bath, a warm hearth, a warm anything at all. If only there were another way to find it—warmth—that holiest of life's luxuries. Somewhere other than the crimson blood of a fresh kill.

She hasn't stopped speaking. The intoxicated don't need much prodding.

"…you can sit and whine about your life, but most things you have a say in." She wipes her tears away. "I think the key is just doing something about it, and I know that, but I didn't have a say in my brother's death. And people just expect you to get on with it. People, with their white teeth and car payments. Their nice, spotless, garage-kept lives."

"I lost my parents," I say, surprising myself. "Seems like another life."

She inhales, stares. "I—I'm sorry. I had no idea how to react at my brother's funeral. I just stared at the shell that was, wasn't, and *used* to be Michael. He looked more peaceful than he'd been in his entire life. How did they pass? If you don't mind me asking?"

"Illness."

The lie is automatic.

I see the old Virginian farmhouse now, I think it was 1830—no, 31.

"Someone's outside," Ma said as Pa got in from putting the donkey away. Such a sweet soul, our mother. The epitome of Southern Belle, like you'd find illustrated in some mass-produced textbook. Ma opened the door to someone I couldn't quite see, saying, "Well, of course you can come in, dear. It's frozen out. What kind of question is— "

It was fast. Crawling along the walls, mouth unhinged, fangs bared.

When I woke, it was dark—dark, but the candle still burning on Hannah Grace and I's bedside table. I sat up in bed, staring down at my parents—drained husks of who they once were. Blood everywhere, detailing where they were thrown and dragged along the walls in dark, broad strokes and strewn along the hardwood floor, like the hush of an abandoned church post-black sabbath.

My once-gray nightgown coated in crimson; a dried river of flaked blood running from my neck to my paler-than-usual skin.

Hannah Grace and I faced one another, knees pulled in, like how we used to talk by candlelight after bath and supper. She stared at me, mouthing my name. Her skin was pale, like my own, concern in her eyes, glowing in the darkness. She turned to our bedroom window, the glass and wood bent and shattered outward, where the stranger Ma invited in must have escaped. She tiptoed over our slain parents, as if not to disturb them, and got into bed with me.

I take it most older siblings are like that, when no mother figure is around.

We sat there three days with them, crawling beneath our beds when the sun rose as if by instinct. Its light leaving us exhausted, geriatric, and debilitated as it looked down on us. The yelps of coyotes filling the cracks of the passing days. The risen moon coaxing them in from the Virginian hills when darkness fell. We sat there starving, until one night we dragged Ma and Pa's mangled bodies to the dandelions behind the farmhouse. And when the coyotes came scrounging around, picking at their dead flesh, we found out what we were. Fast, dangerous, feral...things of unholy legend.

"I don't think we're equipped to deal with something so permanent." She glances up from her phone. "I mean, what do you do when you're staring at death like that?"

"Don't blink," I say, as if the answer had been chambered for a millennium. "If you don't use your pain to press forward, you give it fuel to override you."

"But it gives him life," she says, staring at the white bricks of the nightclub. "He's still with me, in a way, when I ache thinking of him."

I'm not sure I'm capable of crying, given what I am, but I think I come close.

"I don't know, maybe life's a song full of more downs than ups, and we just tap our feet until

17 | SCOTT J. MOSES

we die. I'm Julia, by the way," she says with a smile, the lines of blackened mascara dry now.

"Alice Ann."

We shake hands, somewhat awkwardly after all that.

"You mentioned a sister?"

"Hannah Grace." I sigh, elbows on my knees, chin in my hands. "We used to lie in an ocean of dandelions when we were little, while Pa plowed the field and Ma hung the clothes to dry in the middle of summer. Trying to match our breathing. Trying to synchronize the rhythm of our hearts. Seems stupid now, but then? Let's just say I haven't felt as alive as I did back then."

"That doesn't sound stupid at all."

"Just seems like a dream…too good to have been true."

Her mouth opens, closes again. She turns to me, says, "Wanna get out of here? I think I'm gonna head home, put on a movie or something. I'm sure my date's long gone. We've been out here awhile."

I see Hannah Grace in her denim jacket, clutching her phone, pacing the length of the big rig, Bodachi yelling inaudible curses at me from the outskirts of the city.

He's gonna kill me.

"I think I'll stay awhile," I say, rising to my feet.

A hand on my arm.

I turn and she extends a receipt, a number scrawled across it in pink lipstick.

"This is me, if you ever wanna talk. Nice meeting you, Alice Ann."

"You as well."

"No, really. Thank you." She's crying again. "Thank you."

I stare at the glistening pavement, take the receipt from her.

"It doesn't stay so dark and dreary," I lie. "And I know you know that, but sometimes, it's nice to hear it from someone else."

She smiles, as her phone flashes her driver's ETA: *3 minutes.*

"You're one of the good ones," she says, and I almost believe her.

A gray Civic pulls up to the rear entrance of the club, and it's then I'm aware of the bass still exploding behind us.

She opens the rear passenger door, spins around, smiles, and forms a phone with her pinkie and thumb. Mouths: *Call me.*

The door closes, and the sedan sputters off.

Interesting night.

I beat on the club's back door, and the rhinoceros cracks it ajar.

"You can't come in this—"

I flash him my band.

"Miss, you have to re-enter from the fro—"

I meet his eyes.

"Open, says me."

He does. Of course he does.

At the bar, Julia's *match* has his head in his hands. Hair more disheveled than ever, the crowd still a churning ocean of multicolored lights. The pounding bass a metronome.

The barman walks over, pouring red syrup into a tall glass filled with orange liquid.

"Your brother's done. I should've kicked him out a while ago."

"I appreciate that, I really do. Maybe next year, buddy." I clap my arm around his shoulder and pause, address the bartender again. "What's that you're making?"

"Tequila Sunrise," he says, replacing the smaller bottle beneath the bar.

Of course it is.

"Can I get one for the road?"

He raises a brow.

"Sorry, bad phrasing."

He sighs, but the twenty I slide him seems to change his mind.

He fills a tall glass with ice, and I surveil the crowd. Smiles all around. Carefree sheep in carefree skins living carefree lives. But no, perhaps that's not it at all. Maybe this is just them instinctively crawling beneath their beds as dawn brightens a dark sky.

The drink is served in a tall glass, red syrup

trickling down through the orange like blood. My stomach groans, and a sharp pain shoots through me. I need to leave before this becomes an all-you-can-eat buffet.

I bring the drink to my lips and decide that I don't like the taste of the sun. I'm happy with my life, if it can be called that.

Yes, my life.

I replace the cocktail and laugh in that breathy way I did when I was alive. You know, *alive* alive, and throw another ten on the bar. The barman nods, and I rise with my *not-brother*, who struggles on wobbly legs.

"Come on, James," I say, pulling the first name my mind hands me. "Time to go, loser."

My phone buzzes.

Shitshitshit.

Seven texts and a voicemail.

Hannah Grace: Seriously, Alice Ann, what the fuck?

—Sorrysorrysorry getting a box. Bringing you some.

Hannah Grace: Bodachi is pissed.

—I'm sure.

Hannah Grace: Just get back ASAP, you know how he gets.

—Hannah?

Hannah Grace: Uh, yeah?

—I love you. I'm glad I didn't wake up alone that night in Virginia.

Hannah Grace: Love you too. Get home…weirdo.

✝

I smile as we leave, the *match's* and my boots sloshing through the puddles left from the day's earlier rains. My thoughts of the sun, daylight, and warmth left rotting in that thrumming maelstrom.

I wait until we're in the dark of the alley before slinging the sedated sheep over my shoulder, climbing the slick bricks of the nearest brownstone. Clambering for the only warmth I'll ever need.

CHAPTER 2
OF STARS AND HOW THEY DIE

I love when it rains, when it's cold out. Not that I feel anything other *than cold*, but you get my meaning. Make no mistake though, all that UV's still coming down through the shroud of clouds above, despite their obscured, uncaring gaze on us all, but it makes the extra clothing—the hoodie beneath my leather jacket, the gloves, the beanie— less conspicuous. As for the shades on indoors, and lack of pluming air from my all but useless lungs, well, that's something else entirely. See, on grey overcast days I can walk with them, pretend I'm *one* of them. And sure, it's risky—but if those clouds decide in unison to dissipate, if that sun peeks out from behind them spilling out and over me in this quaint Virginian cafe—well, that wouldn't be so bad either.

I clasp my hands around my coffee, wincing from the piercing headache I've had since waking, (been getting them more and more lately), and twist in my chair to face the melancholic street with its brick-laden sidewalks. The blurred rain loosed from the sky cascading down the storefront's glass. A quaint downtown in the state I was born. Good ol'

Virginia. When I'm here, (even after all this time), my accent creeps back in its way…what's it been, Virginia? Three? Four years? I can't honestly say, but this is more than a nostalgic walk alongside memories I'd be better off forgetting. See, one of ours has gone rogue, is being sloppy, and I'm here to balance the scale. They're flashy, likely freshly turned, and it's these types who ruin things for the rest of us. Attention is, well, it's a drag for wranglers, like Bodachi, and my ilk alike. And in this most symbiotic of relationships between conductor and passenger, sometimes we're sent to kill our own when they make trouble. Because trouble for Bodachi, means trouble for Hannah Grace and I. And those who cause trouble for my sister usually die.

The less people know about us—any of it, really—the better. So yeah, Virginia's all abuzz with the recent murder of a young girl. A girl found in an alley in Richmond, with jagged bite marks in her neck. If she was bitten, she died before she turned, well, that or she's screaming from within a wooden box six feet below the earth somewhere. Hell of a way to spend eternity, but slow turns *do* happen, you hear about them now and again.

I bring my fingers to my throbbing temples. *Another headache, wonder if I'm coming down with something...* Though, that'd be a first. I'm not sure I'm subject to illness anymore, but Hannah, she's been sick, something I'd never thought possible, staying behind more and more while I hunt for the two of us. She rarely leaves the rig, and is *always* with Bodachi. There's something that's been on the cusp of my mind lately, waiting to spill over. It calls to me. What's wrong with her? What could—

And here it is again. This glimmer of some half-remembered dream. Something tangible, corporeal, and yet, foreign. Hannah Grace on the bed. The room's periphery distorted so I can't make out much, but Bodachi's there... He looks at me, smiles. Hannah Grace nibbles her bottom lip, opens her mouth, says—

Two paws rattle the storefront glass and I spook, spilling coffee on my sleeve and the cafe bar. My dead heart stutters, forcing the stilled blood through my stagnant veins, attempting to revive itself. Reminding me of what could still be... or just moving the stagnation forward for no other reason than it is there to be moved.

The yellow lab's owner, a man in wrap-around earmuffs and in a long tan coat, jerks the leash of the still-barking, ravenous Labrador, and waves in apology at me through the glass while the big oaf pulls the leash taut. I don't reciprocate the gesture, and as they pass, the dog glances over its shoulder at me as it rounds the corner. A snarl on its curled, drooling lips. I actually like dogs, but hell knows they don't like me.

"Now, what did you say to upset a good boy like that?" asks a dark-haired girl two seats over, an earbud between the tips of her fingers and sitting before a laptop. She smiles, pushes her tortoise glasses up on her face.

I don't know what to say, and even after these weeks of giving an honest effort, talking with humans is still—strange.

She smiles, opens her mouth to speak as her phone *dings* by her coffee.

NEW MATCH

I glance from it to her. She notices.

"Oh, don't judge," she says, and tucks the phone into the computer bag slung across her chair's back. "The dream of meeting someone organically is dead."

She goes back to her typing, and I lift my nose to the window again. The scent is faint, but *there*. My kind can smell one another once we're close enough. Think it akin to bears pissing on trees to mark their territory. A rugged, rustic smell lost on humans.

One thing the wranglers have going for them is their vast network of communication. Each rig is a set of eyes and intel. It isn't just that he's sloppy, no…this one wronged them somehow, that much I know, though I didn't ask how. Hell, I needed an excuse to get out in the half-light. It's been a while.

She turns back to her laptop, scrolling through an article about stars, sips her coffee. My lips curl in a smirk. I've told myself I'll try harder to converse with them, those I'm still so jealous of.

I turn to her, coffee in hand as the static rain sings

beyond the glass. "You know Astrology's a scam, right?" I sip my coffee as her eyes meet mine. "I mean, I get the appeal though. It's easier to neglect responsibility if you blame everything on the stars."

She smiles, chuckling with her entirety, shoulders shaking as she twists to me. My sister laughs like that. A full body thrum, as if the joy's boiling over, and forcing an exit. I've never understood it.

"So, when were you born?" she asks, voice higher now, bobbing her head side-to-side like some K-pop video, and despite the stupidity of it all, I think back *to those hot summers lying with Hannah Grace in the field behind our quaint Virginian farmhouse, and find I can't remember. I only recall being born that second time... When the drifter, though invited, desecrated our home, my happiness, and sunk his teeth into my sister and I. Me sitting up in bed when it was done, Hannah Grace's eyes glowing in the twilight. Our parents slain and twisted on the floor between our beds.*

"Summer," I say, clasping my coffee, bringing it to my lips again, eyes on a passing red sedan.

"You know this isn't Astrology, right?" And there's something gone from her words now.

She was being sarcastic... When did you get so dense, Alice?

She doesn't miss a beat. "*This* is Astronomy, *actual* science. For example—" She turns her screen to me. It reads: *How 40,000 Tons of Cosmic Dust Falling to Earth Affects Us All.* "This is an article on dying stars," she continues, enraptured by the glowing monitor now. "You're referring to Horoscopes, the Zodiac and all that—which are fine in their own right, thank you very much."

I smirk, lift a hand in defense. A pigeon bobs along the sidewalk behind the glass at my boots, pecking the chipped walkway on occasion.

Her typing stops. "Besides, what's wrong with believing in something? It's that, or admit there's nothing, right? That it's all meaningless." She shuts her laptop, removes her earbuds. "Let's say nothing matters. Given that we're here in spite of that, wouldn't doing the things we love be a kind of rebellion? A miracle even? I think making meaning is an alchemy we don't give ourselves enough credit for."

A club outside Boston flashes in my mind. An alley, a drunk swaying girl. Her smile. Her scent. The weight of her scrawled number still in my breast pocket. A leaden mass there ever since.

Nostalgia escapes me in a sigh.

"I met someone like you once," I say, sipping my coffee, tasting nothing. "But what I'd ask her, and what I'll ask you now, is say you live forever. Where's the meaning then?"

She pauses, and once idle water skids up onto the sidewalk from a passing car.

She turns to me, spark of something in those eyes. Deadly serious, though smiling. "Well, we don't now, do we…and that's what gives this—" she spreads her arms over the cafe— "Meaning. Value."

My stomach drops. My peripheral fears confirmed. Her words cut harder than she knows.

She blows into her coffee's lid, takes a sip. "How many dead stars do you think you're made of?" She looks to the ceiling, a finger tapping her cup to the beat of Bob Dylan's words through the overhead speaker. "I like to imagine me as a thousand burning stars. The cosmic debris in my blood and guts and brain keeping me alive. Fueling—no, *comprising* my soul. It's just so…"

I miss the rest. The scent is strong now, almost physical in its pungency. Through the storefront glass, a man in a long slate-colored coat and fedora, rounds the corner of the glum downtown street. I inhale him, clock the shades over his eyes. He's something out of a Noir film, but there's no doubt about it. He reeks of death and rancid decay, like me. This is my boy.

The Astronomer's still going on, oblivious to my ignoring her. She pushes her glasses up on her nose again, scrolling through another article, and when she turns to me, my gaze envelops her. Her pupils dilate, lip trembling, as she slackens in her chair. I lean in, head throbbing in a pulse now, still clocking the passing ronin in my peripheral vision. "The man walking along the street." She turns to him, mouth slightly ajar, drool forming in the corner of her lips.

"Oh, okay…" Her words slur like a drunk.

Another car passes in a whir as the man waits at a nearby crosswalk. He looks skyward at the rain's recent uptick.

"Go to him, say you're a bit of parlay. If he misunderstands, say you're a gift from a like-minded individual. An olive branch. Then, arm in arm, walk six blocks down Main, turning left at the final light where downtown begins to thin. There's an abandoned brick house, visible from the intersection, condemned, windows shattered, and with an enormous pine in its front yard. Lead him around back and to the basement hatch, coax him inside."

She nods, pushing her chair back with such force that it falls to the floor with a *thwack*. The bell chimes as she leaves behind her every possession. Such a good girl.

I watch her cross the street without looking, an SUV having to slow a bit to allow her by. She intercepts the man at the crosswalk. They converse, and after a while, she takes his arm. The two of them strolling down Main like new lovers.

I massage my screaming temples. The pain angrier than before. Pretty big ask when it comes to hypnosis, but I've done longer. I remove the flask from my jacket, turn it back as the gray outside looses a barrage of slanting rain.

"Um," a voice behind me now. "You can't drink in here." A barista stands at the edge of the cafe's small counter. The few patrons scattered throughout the room turn, look to me as well.

Johnny Cash's "Ain't No Grave" flows from the speakers. The raspy voice coaxing me in thought. It dawns on me to tear them apart, rip them limb from limb, but Bodachi says the initial response to confrontation is usually the wrong one. And so, replacing the flask, I rise from my chair, glimpse the now empty crosswalk, and lifting my still steaming coffee, I shoot it down in one gulp. Their eyes widen, and a transfixed man drops his latte to the floor. The bell sings as I push the door open with a smirk. Hannah Grace shaking her head in my mind.

I adjust my Ray Bans as I round the corner of the dilapidated house, the frames crawling down the bridge of my nose in the slick rain. The twin metal doors to the house's bowels lay splayed, open wide as if they're the unhinged jaw of some serpent, peering up from the earth, mouth ajar in anticipation.

Maybe the basement was a bad call...

Fingers flexing, I roll my neck, the bones cracking therein. I haven't fought one of ours in a long while, and hell knows that this wolf's gotten lazy picking off easy sheep for so long—here's hoping it's the same story for him.

The decrepit steps groan beneath my boots, the exhaled dust of each a whisper when it caresses the concrete below. A rapid heartbeat thrums in my ears, pulsing in my skull, though the blood from my flask sustains me.

Nice thinking, Bodachi.

It's dark but for the sliver of grey crawling through the lone window in the corner. The Astronomer is prostrate, groaning there on the floor, her breaths shallow, fingers, arms, and legs, twitching. Blood pools from her head, and her hair sticks to the concrete, flat and matted with crimson.

I suck in the scent of my kind and turn to the rusted water heater under the stairs. My right hand's fingers extend, and the cracked sheep nails dislodge, give way for elongating claws. "Come out, or I'll drag you out by your tongue."

He stirs, slowly rising, peculiar look on his sunken face. He steps out as if entranced, drunk even. Five o'clock shadow peppers his face, dark circles as chasms beneath his tired eyes, *heart slamming in his chest.*

Human, and yet…something's there…familiar…

He runs a hand through his greasy hair. "I hardly believe it," he says, standing in the grey allowed from the window. "They said it would draw you out. That you or yours would find me, something about the smell…"

He digs the metal fangs from atop his sheep's teeth, points at me. "Your eyes, they glow like coins. Like the forums said."

"Whom do you serve?" I say, biting my lip to murder a half-formed smirk. The saying is well-traveled, comical in these modern times, but Familiars, Thralls, they're usually desperate, take their jobs seriously.

He relaxes, shifting his weight to his other leg.

He's rife with our stench. "Whom do I *serve*?" I clock the crowbar in his other hand. "Well, all of you, really."

I step towards him, flexing my left hand, watching him watch the claws sprout from my pale fingertips. "Does your master hibernate? Too weak to hunt?" *I hate the idea of killing a vegetable in its sleep, but so it goes.* "Your killings—you're being sloppy—gonna get caught. And I *like* Virginia. I plan on coming back."

"So you," he says with a smile, bloodshot eyes gleaming. "You include me?"

The girl groans on the floor near the cinder block wall, dragging her arm in stuttered arcs along the floor.

He moves to her, and I allow it. "The blood's working…like he said it would." He steps on the exploring arm, halting its motion. "Her eyes were *large, dilated* when I spoke to her." He turns to me, smile wider than it rightly should be. "I think I hypnotized her. I'm beginning to see now that in my world, all things eventually work to my benefit." He casts a hand over the girl like she's roasted, apple in her mouth. "The killings are an offering to *you*, your *kind*. You're gods in this world, but so am *I*, and I'm awake now, moving lucid through my creation."

"Like *who* said it would? How do you carry our scent? Whom do you—"

"No," he says, voice deeper now, grip wrenching the crowbar. "I've waited too long for this—have questions." The girl's fingers curl beneath his weight. The sun seeping in through the dirtied window in the upper corner.

"Well," I say, removing my shades, staring into him. Loosing the hooks of my mind. "I've questions too. Whom….do…you…serve…?"

He twitches and blood spurts from his nose. He shakes his head, chuckles. "I don't think that works on me anymore. I'm like you now, or close enough. A god of gods in this world."

"Says the man in fake fangs…." I try again with all I am, and he backs to the wall from the force of my mind. A knife sheaves through my undying brain with the effort, and I fall to a knee. Something cool runs from my right ear. I wince, growling. "What do you mean *the blood*?"

Red runs in tributaries from his nose and lips. "I injected it," he slurs, swaying. "It speaks to me. Says I'm the dreamer…creator."

I rise, my brain screaming with the exertion, aflame with pain. "Whom do you *serve*?"

He wipes the blood from his face, trembling again. "Why, I serve *all*, Upir. I give this world *life*."

He's insane. Strung out on…something…

"What's it like?" he asks, leaning forward, both hands gripping the crowbar so tightly it shakes. "Living forever without fear. The things you can do."

"Some days it's like Sisyphus and his stone." My fingers twitch, anticipating violence. "Living forever, well, it gets old."

The dreamer rolls his neck, shifting his gaze to

the girl who's long since stopped moving, his mouth ajar. A string of bloody drool descends in a line to the floor by his shoes. He smiles, and replacing his fake fangs, blood pools from his mouth, down his chin.

"I know your kind," I say, watching him loom over her. "Killing for sport."

He whips around, eyes wide. Blood seeping between the spaces of his gritted teeth. "This was for *you*. An offering to meet one of *you*." He points to the motionless astronomer. "*She* said as much. We're *in my dream, Upir*. All things work to my benefit here. This place *is me*, and *I* am *it*, as are *you*. And in you being me and I manifesting you, well, I know we kill for the same reasons."

"I kill to survive."

He chuckles. "Though, you enjoy it."

A drunken boy abducted from a club just south of Boston. The power I'd felt that night. Bending them all to my will, all but one...her. The look on Bodachi's face when I drew near, the sheep slung across my shoulder. Hannah Grace showing the first signs of her weakness, staying behind while I had a night on the town.

He's still talking.

"I've come to in a dream of my own making. The blood has shown me...*continues* to do so...and you, standing there so sure of yourself before a god. Though why wouldn't you be? You're gods in this world of mine. But how can you be sure of anything? It's belief which makes us conscious." He stumbles towards me, his eyes different now, one more dilated than the other. The right side of his face droops like a stroke victim. "Observing the world through those two indentions above your nose."

I've had enough. "Sorry, but I'm real as day, if you'll pardon the expression." I curl my fingers, widen my gait in a subtle crouch. "Tell me, if you die in your dream…what happens then?"

He relaxes his posture. "You wouldn't, not now that you know what I am. *Who* I am. See, if you kill me, if I were to wake, this, you, all of it goes away…so I've been murdering and killing these women in hopes that your ilk would find me, give me life eternal, so that in *me* living forever, *you* might as well in this world I've created. This world I've dreamt for us all."

I move how only my kind can. Breaching the gap between us in too few strides. I yank his hair and head aside, expose his pulsing throat, whisper, *"Wakey, wakey,"* and plunge my teeth into his jugular. Real fangs doing real work. I'm full, but I don't care. I'm angry, alive and dead all at once.

Me and Hannah Grace as children in our family's field. Back when we waved sticks as swords in autumn before we were called in for supper, before the grass turned to dust, the soil to ash.

I pull myself from him, and plunge my clawed fingers through his jacket, skin, and flesh. Tearing past the moist innards, and as my hand juts upward, snapping ribs and ligaments with its ascension, I grasp his quick-thrumming heart. Blood juts from him with the movements, gravity feeding on the mess pouring from his torso. He's terrified, bulging eyes agape, pleading for his end, but the notion that he *might* be to blame takes root, spurs me on.

All of this—my life, Hannah's, her sickness, our slain parents—could've possibly been avoided if he hadn't dreamt it, made it into being.

Blood launches from his mouth as I grip his heart tighter, speaking to divinity if it ever existed.

"Why create? Why birth the possibility of pain?"

As his heart collapses I can't help but moan. Because of what he thinks he is, wants to be. Because coattails weren't made to be ridden. And it's the closest thing to killing God I've ever known.

I pull my arm free, and he collapses at my feet, sheep that he is.

"Human," I say, as if the very word's derogatory, beneath me, and yet, there it is….that familiar tang of jealousy after each kill. The opportunity to die, and how it's lost on my sister and I. Stolen from us by someone whose face I barely remember.

I fall to my knees, looking down on the dead man, his overcoat streaked crimson and in disarray. Limbs splayed as if he's fallen from a great height.

And there it goes, as it always does. That most foreign of invaders clawing throughout my entirety. How my throat tightened before my hand went searching for his soul. That unfamiliar feeling come 'round now and again, if even that often: hope. To latch onto the dream's orator, kill its master, and fade into oblivion…that was the promise made in this condemned husk of a once home. All humans do is lie, and I can't help but smile at my continued belief in them all.

I rise, glowering over him a moment before I crush his neck with my boot, lest he get his wish. His head lolls, free-floating, detached from his spine. Something resembling a billfold peeking out at me from his inner jacket's pocket. I pluck it free, unfolding the leather in the lowlight.

A syringe, spare needles, and two vials: one empty, one full of red. I bring the filled vial close, pop the lid, inhale. The scent is putrid, lined with decay, blood, yes, but void of life. He'd injected it, and if there was once a sound mind within the walls of his skull it had robbed him of it.

I replace the cap and tuck the vial into my jacket pocket, tossing the leather case aside.

Sun's stare fills the window now, illuminating the once-concealed dust floating on the air. The light rests on the girl's face. She moans.

Alive? But I push the thought away. I need to leave, show Bodachi and Hannah Grace what I've found. As I make for the stairs, I'm taken back to the last night of my life. The one I'd give what little's left of me to forget. I clutch the railing, and look to her there, so helpless. My mother in her place now, broken and drained. Her pale skin waxy, her thin veins constricted and pushing out from the taut skin of her face. I still question why Ma and Pa didn't turn. Why we at least couldn't still be a family if forced to exist like this. She groans again, and I imagine myself the drifter, standing before some girls' bedroom window, looking over a shoulder at my work, the slain, my yellowed fangs long as railroad spikes.

The old railing cracks in my grasp, and I look to the open hatch-doors above, willing myself to them. I ascend the protesting steps, and pulling on the hood of my sweatshirt, I half emerge from the doors clothed in the shade of some nearby pines, and grasping a door with each hand from the stairs, I pull them shut.

I bend to her and her shallow breaths, brush the hair from her throat. There's a faint imprint of a soul extinguished within me, and though I'm a husk staring through endless grey from the dark of this world's corners, there's something *there*, waiting for a glimpse of who I was, *wanting* to remember. Every now and then, it comes up for air.

As fangs break skin and warmth fills my mouth, I'm lost in thought. It's not often I have time to contemplate things. Why we do what we do, or how we go about doing it. The way I see it? If we have to be bad to survive, why can't we be a little good doing so?

Rather than swallow, I expel the blood back with my saliva (The secret spice, if you will), and slumping against the cinder block wall, I pull her head into my lap, cradling it there, her eyes darting behind closed lids.

Up to you now, Astronomer.

The rays of that burning sun creep through the soiled glass above us, and it dawns on me to steal a caress. Going as far as to extend my hand to its majesty, fingers outstretched. *A memory now: me running my hands through the golden grain of my family's field. The sun's on my face. It's warm, so warm.* I close my eyes in the half-dream, and as the eternal cold of my existence drives the memory from me, I clench them tighter, grasping at its receding aura, willing its return, attempt to weave a dream of my own.

I rap on the motel room's door. "Hey, you ready?"
The sun hides behind the grey melancholia above the truck stop. I'd crawled from my place in the eighteen-wheeler, between the pallets of animal feed and manure, things to keep the curious away. At his most paranoid, Bodachi loads the trailer with raw fish, anything to throw off, well, everyone. Sometimes I wonder if we wouldn't be better off in the sewers of some high-life metropolis like others we've met along the way.

I knuckle the door again, and the curtain drawn across the window shivers. Movement. *A car passes behind me in the near-lifeless parking lot, though*

I'm not worried. The motel and stop are both wrangler owned. I knock again. Pause. Harder now. Nothing.

I grip the doorknob, twist, feel it protest. The motel's buzzing sign at the turn-off flashes through my mind: **Welcome Inn.** *And as the cheap lock buckles with more persuasion, I push open the door.*

Hannah Grace sits on the bed, back against the cheap headboard. Her eyes meet mine, and she winces as if pained at my entry. Bodachi's in a chair next to her, his hands steadying a syringe and its plunger. He pauses his withdrawal, and the red swarming the translucent plastic from the crook of Hannah's arm does as well. He goes white, despite his olive complexion, and removes the syringe. His head jerks to Hannah, though her gaze doesn't leave mine, red wells in her glassy blues. I realize my jaw's dropped, find Bodachi's widening eyes.

"What?" I ask, and flex the fingers of my right hand. "What are you doing, Bodachi?"

He stands, stumbling back into the nightstand. A lamp topples from its surface and falls to the floor. Its bulb still glowing in the silence.

He backs to the wall, blindly feeling his way as he goes, his eyes stuck to mine. I've never seen him like this before. "Go on, Hannah," he says, reaching for the snub nose he keeps in the small of his back. "Now."

Blood runs like tears from Hannah Grace's eyes, her lip trembles.

"I can't..." she says, crimson veins in webs now.

"Not aga—"

"Hannah!" Bodachi screams, even as I'm stepping towards him, fangs extending over my lip, the nails of my right hand grown long. Hannah speaks, stills me dead when our eyes meet.

"Alice," she says, and her eyes dilate. The talons of her mind laying siege to my innermost self.

I slacken, falling back against a dresser at the foot of the bed. Malformed versions of words leaving my lips. "We...have to go. He's close..."

Bodachi relaxes, his hand moving from the still tucked revolver, and righting the fallen chair, he's at her side again. He massages her upper arm, and upon the syringe's reinsertion, blood floods the barrel again.

"I'm not coming," Hannah says, her voice quivering. "I'm...not well." Her eyes widen, and my knees all but buckle. "You have to forget this, okay? You were never here." She wipes away bloody tears, red smearing her cheeks. "Go get him, Alice."

Bodachi mumbles something I don't quite catch. Prick? Thief?

I sway in a stupor, and turn for the door, catching myself on its frame. "Sure, feel better." I grip the door with an unsteady hand, glance over my shoulder.

"Bodachi?"

He looks up at me, stiffening in the chair as if caught, guilty. "What, girl?"

Drool slides from the corner of my mouth with the words. "Take care of her."

With a long sigh, he nods, smiling as his heart rate slows, resuming his default demeanor, calm, Zen. "'Course, it's me, Alice." He leans towards me and his eyes flick to Hannah before he meets my drunken gaze. He smiles, says, "Tear his heart out, girl."

Hannah Grace points to the sunglasses at my boots, I pluck them up and...I'm seated at the cafe's bar, watching a man and his yellow lab turn the corner a few blocks up Main. It's raining, I'm—

I lurch forward in a fury, hyperventilating with the recollection. Sucking in the musty air solely out of habit, reflex. Seems panic warrants akin reactions from the living and the dead. My chest and ribs crack, pop, violently reawakened.

She made me forget...like a sheep...but how? Why...?

I pull the filled vial from my pocket, bring it close to my eyes, twirl it there. I pop the cap with my thumb nail, bring it to my nostrils.

Why give your blood?

I remove my burner from my inner pocket and flip it open as headlights pass over the windowpane above. The old glass glistens, some far off, abstract universe glimpsing our own.

My thumbs hover over the keys. Hannah's name in bold atop the blank canvas of a text I can't seem to form.

How long has this been going on?
And I thought I was hiding things.
Liar.

Why not tell me?

My eyes fall to the vial, then to the dreamer's corpse propped up near me, the jagged punctures in his throat.

"Tell me more," I whisper to the blood. "Help me remember."

I shoot the crimson down like it's cheap whiskey, there to perform a function and not to be enjoyed.

The empty vial rolls from my fingers, stops where the wall meets the concrete. A shifting in my lap. A tremor. She's looking up at me, eyes gleaming like galaxies, skin paler than it's been or will ever be. She draws in breath, wriggling her nose at the discomfort. At the once automatic function become manual, unnecessary.

I clench my teeth behind my lips, brace for the onslaught. For all the questions I've heard so much about. All the *hows, whys,* and *what nows?* The mysterious ocean Hannah Grace and I had to navigate ourselves. Our maker just another absent father in a world of absent fathers.

She tilts her head. A swaddled newborn with a spinning mobile. "Your eyes…"

Guilt surges through me. That's one thing I still feel. It's always there, deep down where the marrow used to be. Perhaps that's all I am now: walking guilt, selfish longing, insatiable regret.

She curls in on herself, and her stomach groans. She winces, teeth and eyes clenched.

Her hand levitates, floating toward the dreamer's corpse not far from us. She sits forward, though I doubt she knows why, and I stay her ascension, easing her back down.

"Can't drink from the long dead," I say, and she's lost in my eyes again. The intimacy a house aflame. "Doesn't work that way."

She shivers, takes in her surroundings with a slow, swiveling head. I remember the utter calm now, the complete serenity of waking to pseudo-life from the dream that *was* your life. Doesn't last though. Nothing does.

I wring my stomach out like a rag, forcing the dreamer's—*Hannah's*—blood back up, my mouth filled with it. I kiss my index finger and its tip comes back red. I lower it to her. She sniffs, and her eyes widen.

Her tongue darts out, sapping the blood from my finger, and life enters her, those brown eyes brighter than before. She looks to me, the dreamer's corpse, and finally to the window above us in the what should-be—used-to-be-for-her-not-so-long-ago— darkness.

"Am I…" she begins, not knowing how. "Am I dead?"

A lump forms in my throat, and despite having the answer I'm at a loss. She wipes her drowsy eyes, and I glimpse her bracelet. Emblazoned in the thin metal are two words: *"Embrace Uncertainty."*

She curls in on herself again, arms cradling her stomach.

Hannah and I in agony, hunched and gritting our teeth, dragging our parents atop the bloodied hardwood of our no-longer-home. The yelps of the coyotes making the hunger in us furious.

I purge my stomach, angling her mouth beneath mine, and pinch her nostrils shut. The old instinct, though irrelevant now, kicks in, and her mouth opens for air. She struggles at first, grabbing my elbow with her thin fingers, but when the blood comes, dripping slow like molasses to her tongue, she relaxes, coos even, swallowing it down like it's the best thing she's ever had, because it *is*.

I lean back, lick the blood from my lips, and she wipes her mouth and chin with her fingers. Sucks them dry like a baker's asked her to clean the spoon. She glances to the steps.

"I need to get back," she says, foot still in her old life. "My astronomy final's tomorrow. I need to study."

Thanks to the delirium of the change, she hasn't even questioned how she got here. If there's a time to tell someone that life as they know it has ended, it's now.

I open my mouth to speak and pause with realization: *I never asked her name. She who was once a tool, a means to my end, now my responsibility. How the clouds lie heavy in this mess I've made.*

"What's your name?"

She creeps onto her elbows. "Imani," she says, and massaging her forehead, she lies back down, her body unacclimated to the change.

I brush the blood-matted hair from her face. "There's no going back now, Imani, at least not that I've found."

"What do you...what do you mean?"

I look to the ceiling, the exposed studs there. "You're like those dead stars now." Rain taps the window in increasing fervor. "Stay too close to the living and you'll swallow them up."

She looks to consider this, big browns bouncing from the dreamer to me, the window, me again. I can't imagine what Bodachi will do. Maybe I'll play like she was already turned... but no... she'll have questions, the answers to which are learned in the first nights of being what we call "alive."

"There's," she begins, startling me from thought, "something inside you."

That's nothing you sense. A heavy void, and it's in you now too. That's the soul fading from your shell. I should've let you die...

She looks up at me again, eyes twinkling in the blue dark, fear overtaking her features.

I don't *need* to breathe, but occasionally I will to remember what it feels like. To gorge on the air as my neglected lungs engage in their old way. Recalling a farm in Virginia, my life before...warmth. Trying to recall our donkey's name, a name Hannah and I can't seem to remember. The time I fell from him. Pa's laugh. My mother's smile. Hannah Grace in that motel room. How she made me forget. Bodachi's smile of approval—*relief* at the act, and as rumination takes hold, jagged questions swarming my mind, I return to the breath. To the present moment, lowering my gaze to the newborn.

"Do something for me, Imani."

Our eyes meet, though she doesn't speak.

"Inhale and think on your life. Of those closest to you. The ones you love most. Savor the breath, remember, and never forget what it was to be alive."

Her face is blank. She parts her lips to speak.

"Go on," I say. "You'll thank me later."

She closes her eyes, sucking in the air. The once automatic action requiring conscious effort now, like scratching a non-existent itch. I wonder what she's thinking, watching her there in my lap, little knowing she'll often revisit this moment. Replaying it over and over. How this memory—*all* memories—are just copies of what truly occurs. A clone of a clone transfigured and slowly altered over time.

Her eyes move from behind her lids as if dreaming, and in a way, she is. We all are.

My head throbs and I'm taken from the moment's peace to the problem at hand, or rather, my lap.

Hannah Grace charmed me... It shouldn't be possible, and yet, beyond the hows, lie the whys?

Questions rear their heads, roaring in the stillness, but above the chaos a soft voice mumbles.

The Astronomer's eyes reveal themselves, and I brace myself for more questions, how she'll take the answers.

She swallows. "How many dead stars are you made of…?"

I rest my head against the cinder block wall, Hannah's scent thick on the musty air. And gazing up at the exposed studs and piping, the bones of this sad, sorry place, the words catch in my throat, claw free: "Just the one."

CHAPTER 3
OUR OWN UNIQUE AFFLICTION

The rush of the swaying grass all around me, obscuring my view. Like the waters of some vitriolic river. Amused at my folly. The roar a million insects in flight, an applause, as the wind picks up again. The breath ripped from my lungs, I lie there, my mouth opening and closing, gasping for air, looking up at the uncaring, unapologetic face of our donkey. He's chewing something, those big brown eyes taking me in, as if he *knows* what he's done. A scream in the distance then, atop the wind.

"Alllllliiiiiicccceeee! Aliiiiicccceeee!"

Hannah?

The field falls away, and it all goes dark. I wonder if this is oblivion. It's blacker than I've seen in a long while. I'm lying down, crumpled into myself. A searing pain in my head and guts forces my knees to my chest. I hiss, cry out. I haven't fed since the dreamer, but how long ago was that? Days? *Weeks*? Time is irrelevant in the dark. It's colder than usual, and I'm *always* cold.

The click of a lighter behind me. The wavering light cascades up the wall, revealing the bars of my cage. The shimmering flame reflected on the inside of the rig's trailer.

How...what's—

The smell of nicotine on the air. An exhale, someone laughs through their nose.

"You know," a rusty voice says from behind me. "I've heard of this, but seeing it's something else."

I roll over and searing pain churns through my bones. The hurt an echo throughout me, a pulsing agony stemming from my stomach. Leaning against the wall is someone I've seen before but can't place where. One of those *here and theres* you can never pin down.

"Bodachi's—" I cough, my throat raw, as if charred. I coil again, straightening when the pain passes. "Not usually one for company."

The trailer's empty, which is a first, and glancing down its length, I note the wide-open doors, their display. *Night, stars, the tips of pines, a guard rail.*

"Lending a hand to an old friend is all," he says, taking a drag from his cigarette. "And I couldn't be *happier* to. I mean, seeing you, *any of you*, like this, after hunting us for so long?" He chuckles and looks to the ceiling in pseudo-thought. "What's the old adage? Pride coming before the fall?"

I corkscrew as unseen hands wrench my innards, hissing as if branded, my teeth clenched.

I remember leaving the basement. Me carrying Imani halfway to the wrangler's motel, then, nothing...

Agony melts to a simmer, and I tune into his words.

"...fucked up, really. And how funny is it that after all that, after all those centuries living in fear, you came crawling to *us*. Needed something only we could give as the night lit up with lights, burning away the dark you and yours had hidden away in so long."

He pulls on his cigarette and the embers illuminate his person. A leather pilot's jacket, jeans, and a revolver at his hip. Long-sheathed knife strapped to his opposite thigh above combat boots.

I brace for another wave though it doesn't come, and tilt my head up from its sideways angle. "Why are you here...?"

He kicks off the wall, places the cigarette in his teeth. "Oh yeah. Thanks for reminding me." His hand rests on his revolver. He sees *me* seeing *it*, *wants* me to see, says, "I bet this wouldn't kill you normally, slow you down, maybe, but that's about it." He unholsters the weapon, silver gleaming in the moonlight invading the trailer. "But now?" He ejects the wheel, examines its contents. "You're *weak* now."

He locks in the wheel with the flick of his wrist, pulls back the hammer, trains it on me.

Finally...

His shoulders shake, his laughter echoing throughout the trailer. "Awh...so old, yet so gullible." He disengages the hammer and holstering the pistol, he bends for his knife. "Just toying with you, you know, how you toy with *us*?"

He unsheathes it, takes a drag from the cigarette

between his lips, and slices his palm. He extends it to me.

I'm on my belly, spun around, attempting to force my arms through the bars, clawing for the blood *tap tap tapping* on the floor. *So hungry.* I slam my head against the bars, once, twice, again, the metallic clang echoing throughout the corridor. I slump, shoving my lips against the bars near the floor. My tongue extending for the sweet crimson mere feet away.

He chuckles while wrapping the wound in a long bandage, and pulling it taut, he lifts the red jug I'd missed, douses the blood. The scent dissipates, and the room undulates darkness. Exhaustion barrels into me like a colliding moon, and I slump onto my belly, arm half through the gaps in the bars. Cheek pressed to the floor. *So heavy.* My bones iron rods. My muscles mounds of lead.

He sets the jug down by his feet. "Gotta say, girl, I'm surprised, but you haven't eaten in *how* many days now? We'll bleed you of that fight. That's a promise."

I'm breathing, though I don't know why, and as he hefts the jug, walking toward the open doors, I open my mouth to speak. It takes everything to produce sound.

"Where's Hannah…?"

He turns around, looking me dead in the eye. *The ultimate insult.* And as I try to breach his mind, my stomach screams. I wince, hissing there, trembling. The heaviness of sleep crawls over me, but I like sleep. It gets me out of here for a while.

"God," he says, as he blurs in my vision. "She really did a number on you, huh?"

I'm on my back. The ocean of grass and dandelions closing in all around me. Looking up at the flared nostrils of the donkey, teeth chewing nothing much. It rears its head, looks off across the field. The grass sways, applauds.

"Allllllliiiiicccccceeee!"

I lift my head, lungs wrenching, I can't inhale. The impact from the fall still fresh in my bones. I open my mouth, try to breathe, to scream—nothing. The donkey shakes its head, snorts, and walks off. Someone's tunneling through the field behind me. I chomp at the air. A fish baking on sizzling rocks.

Breathe, have to breathe.

Hannah Grace breaks through the grass to my right, stumbling as she sees me, dandelion seeds stuck to her dusted dress. Her big blues are wide, her mouth hangs open.

"Alice," she cries. "Alice, say something."

I claw at my collar, my vision rippling. The field meeting the sky in a hushed medley. My throat tightens, though my chest rises, falls, rises, the breaths no more than wheezes, rapid.

She waves her arms, jumping again and again. The thuds of heavy boots, the grass parting for the man in dirtied clothes, wrinkled, brown hat atop his head. Pa looks down on me, the worry in his face as newly dug trenches.

"Pa, she won't breathe," Hannah Grace says, tears welling and red-faced. Pa cradles my head in his hands. His face and hat enveloping the sky. Those kind grey eyes, his peppered brown beard.

"We're gonna sit up now, hun." And before I know it, I'm upright. The grass doesn't seem so tall now, their whispers less conspiratorial.

"Look at me, Alice," he says, and tears blur my vision, my throat constricting. Hannah Grace cries beside us, and her face fills me with dread. *Hopeless*. As everything closes in, it dawns on me I can't feel my hands. Pa directs my frantic eyes to his own, puts a hand on his chest. "Follow me, girl. Breathe…"

His breaths are s*low, heavy, loooong*, and though wheezing, though panic swarms my entirety, I mimic him. A long wheezing with each exhale. The inhalations as breathing through a nail hole. My lungs expand, and though my chest and neck are still taut, I'm breathing, albeit barely.

I open my mouth, heart slamming in my child's chest, and despite my efforts at sound, the words come in a whisper.

"Pa…" The sun looms bright above, as I gag on strangled words. *"I'm afraid…"*

He sighs and wipes his forehead. Tears welling in his eyes now. They glisten as he speaks.

"That's good, honey," he says, as they carve

canyons through the dust on his face. "That means you're *alive*, means you want to stay that way. Now breeeeeeeathe..."

It's easier now, inhaling as he does, exhaling the same. I'm calmed, and the air comes easier. Hannah Grace isn't crying, not anymore, in fact, she smiles, hands clenching her dusted farm dress.

The wheezing dies away.

Pa leans back, his eyes on the sky, and whispers a prayer I don't catch. He's never had to stop an attack before. Up until now, it's always been Ma.

I'm smiling too, I can't help it. I'm at peace, can *breathe*. The sun's warmth cascades down on us all. I don't hold back, let it all go, crying and laughing there in the dirt. The dam my eyes constructed collapsed now, hemorrhaged. I wipe my eyes, beaming up at the two of them.

Hannah Grace steps back, inhales, a hand over her mouth. Pa falls backwards, crawls kicking and clawing away from me. He breathes heavy now. Hannah Grace hides behind him, peeking out from over his trembling shoulders.

I wipe my tears away. "Pa?" And there it is, the top of my hand and wrist bathed in crimson. Pa jerks up and yanks Hannah to him. The two of them flee through the grass. I don't give chase, *though I could... Oh, how I could.*

The air is frigid when my eyes open, and I walk down a dirt road. Hills stretch in the distance, tinged blue by the night bathing the countryside. I don't know how long I've been walking, only that I am, and that I'll continue to do so till I find what I'm looking for. Coyote song dances on the wind, or does it? *Where am I? What is this…?*

A coagulation of pines rise in the middle-distance as the road slopes down. There's a two-story house. Quaint, yes, but lived in. Candlelight dances in each window of the small abode. I lick my lips, true teeth quivering.

I rap on the wooden door as the wind lifts my hair, stomach groaning, *longing*. A woman in a nightgown opens the door, blonde hair falling down a shoulder in loose disarray. She smiles and I feign weakness. Shivering there on her doorstep.

"I was passing through and…it's just so cold." I shake for emphasis, arms hugging me. "I saw the candles, was wondering if I—"

Worry falls over her, and she extends her hand. "Well, of course you can come in, dear. It's frozen out. What kind of question is— "

I'm on her, my knees pinning her legs, my fangs lodged into her throat, drinking her down. She struggles beneath me. There's someone at the top of the wooden steps. Their heart races, as does their breath, only spurring me on. I pull from her till the life leaves her eyes, jerking up with the new scent in the room, another pounding heart.

A man in a brown hat and beard stands in the rear doorway, mouth hanging wide. Breath caught in his lungs. I smile, baring my teeth at him, and launch myself not at him, but to the wall nearest me. He screams as I barrel down on him, my hardened nails impaling the thick wood of the farmhouse. I punch a hand through his chest, gripping his spine and jerk him close. Sink my teeth into him. A donkey screams from the barn at the house's rear, and sockless feet pad backward at the top of the stairwell. A young girl, her face an amalgamation of fear and dread, disappears around the corner. The thuds of her echoing footfalls on the floor above me. A door slams.

How I love a chase, to wade through their fear as if it were a hot spring.

I gather my kills—one in each hand—and drag them up the stairs. Knees, elbows, and feet *thud* behind me, but I *want* to be heard. As I round the corner, stifled voices quiet behind the lone shut door. I smirk, and glancing over my shoulder at the dead in tow, realize I've left a trail. Twin rivers curling this way and that atop the dilapidated wood. I clomp to the door and the once small voices crescendo before muting. I release the dead. They crumple to the floor, and grasping the door's straight handle, I yank it from its hinges. I cast the door aside, licking my lips, savoring their screams, and round the corner.

The oldest slides off the bed, stands between me and the younger.

"Don't you touch her!" she says, fists clenched, though teetering. I shift my gaze to the other as if in defiance. The blanket's pulled up to her nose, her brown eyes peeking out from over it. I know her, she's me, or who I *used* to be. I smile, despite *myself,* and enter the room, talons quivering. Lusting with hunger though having just fed. My jaw unhinges, swaying like a pendulum, and as a moan leaves my lips, my tongue lolls. A part of me wants them to run, fight, to do *something* to stop what's coming. Red fills my vision, and as I spring towards Hannah Grace, a duet of screams flood my ears.

Tap, tap, tap...

My lids peel open, cheek still pressed against the thick bars of my cage. The trailer's entrance is bursting with light, and it slows to a crawl mid-way into the enclosure. Something cool kisses my forehead, and glancing upward, I see the wrangler, his revolver pressed to me, blood dripping from his reopened wound. He glowers over me. I turn my head, repositioning the barrel between my eyes, and press my head to it. And despite Hannah, Imani, I whisper. *"Please..."*

I let the guilt wash over me.

He chuckles. "Oh, I'm not gonna kill you. Not yet."

Someone grunts, eclipsing the sun let into the trailer. "The hell are you doing in here?"

The wrangler glances over his shoulder, lifts his hands in an *okay, okay* motion to the one behind him. He holsters his revolver, points at the newcomer. "You just remember you called *me,* yeah?"

The near-silence is palpable, all but the blood still dripping from the wrangler's palm.

"Why don't you get some air, Raeger," the voice booms again. "Leave me with her."

The wrangler, Raeger, points his chin my way. "I wager she's almost there. Another day or so. She didn't even go for the blood." He sighs. "Not like last night. You should've seen her, surprised me."

He walks into the light, and I squint from its fervor. How it shimmers around him in silhouette. I could cry.

A deep voice made soft. "Do you remember when it was that that spark in you died?"

I shift my head to Bodachi, crouched there before the bars. His bulk tight with his hunched posture. Head freshly shaven.

My mouth is dry, lips chapped and raw. I turn back to the light. "Only that it did."

He looks to the sun tunneling in as well, turns back to me, sighs. "You know I see you as a daughter, right?"

I'm four times your age, sheep. But the thought's fleeting. The remnants of some stronger being. I fling different words unto the dark.

"Where's Hannah? The newborn?" I grip the bar with a frail hand. The pain long since overtaken by a lethargy I've never known. "I want to see them...now."

He smirks, leans back. "*There's* that spark, what's left of it anyway..." He sounds, off—sad.

"You're not in a position to be making demands, Alice. You know that, right?" He stands, stretches out, and lifts a finger to the open trailer doors. Birds talk in their unknown language. "Look at that," he says. "*Really* look at it." He lowers his finger. "You're in a bad way, Alice. A real bad way." He faces me. "I can't imagine what it's like for one of you to starve. How the lack of blood brings hallucinations, to live in a dream for a time. The past rushing at you in a maelstrom, your life flashing before your eyes as your body anticipates death." He crouches again. "But I've been on the outside looking in many times, girl. *Many* times. And you've lived a long while, haven't you, Alice?"

A memory, or am I there?

Hannah Grace and I in an absinthe bar in New Orleans. It's night, but of course it is. Bodachi's on business in the Garden District, and so we're on the town, together, how it should be. We sit at a candlelit table in the bar's corner with another of our kind: tall and strapping, his skin dark as a moonless sky. He sips his absinthe, examining his glass as if he can actually taste it—or perhaps, he's remembering its taste. He wears a tall skinny top hat and lifting its bill, he sets his drink down.

"You think I'm joshing now, don't you?" he says, and I look from Hannah, who's homed in on the pianist slamming keys on the small stage a few yards from us. The sheep laughing and dancing, all singing the song in unison, drinks and hands clasped. She smiles, a million miles away.

I pull on my own absinthe. "Joshing? About what?"

He shakes his head, steeples his fingers. "That's the problem with you young bloods, still so distracted by it all." He sips his absinthe again, and I do the same. He's old, this one, and I want a good story. He leans in, his elbow on the table guarding his drink from the world. "I've seen it, one of ours starve. Ain't pretty... The bastard deserved it, sure, but it was damned awful."

Applause roars from the miniature dance floor and I glimpse Hannah clapping too. Her eyes gleam, though I doubt anyone notices. People walk along the bustling street outside the still open door in their own worlds. Hannah gives me a wink and I smirk at her, returning to the old timer downing the rest of his drink.

"So, what'd he do?" I ask.

"Don't matter," he says. "Hell, I'm not even sure I recall...was centuries ago, but what I do remember is that they called it Sun Poisoning. It's—" He smiles up at the server, a young girl, her hair up in a bun, who clears our empties. I think to catch her eyes, tell her we've been waiting all night for our first round and how the service is utterly awful, but I refrain.

She leaves, and the old one removes his top hat, wipes his brow. "See, it's not a desperate, thrashing madness, no. It's conscious insanity. *A slow crawl into the depths of all you are. Reality skips like a record, and if you can't get your foot on something solid, you'll perish within yourself, be your own tomb…"*

"And how do you know all this?" Hannah Grace asks beside me now, skeptical as always.

The old one smiles, though it's sad. "Because I helped the lambs hunt him down…was one myself. They said they'd done it before, dozens of times, took joy in explaining it all to the new recruits to stomp out our fear. Their guild, well, they were making a name for themselves and needed conscripts from the local towns. This mark was a real brute, old school, thralls and everything." He holds up two fingers and points to his eyes, his lips. "That battle made *me."*

I sip my absinthe, and Hannah opens her mouth to speak and pauses, removing her burner from her jean pocket. She flips it open, shoots me a knowing look, and nods to the old one. As I rise as well, the old one catches my hand. "You know the closest way to step into you past?" he says, a sternness in his gaze. "Don't feed. It'll make you see who you really are underneath, below what you've buried. What you're running from." I yank my hand from his grasp, turning for Hannah Grace at the bar's entrance.

"Lost you there, huh, girl," Bodachi says, the light in the trailer different now, less than. More gold than yellow with the passage of time, but *how much* is anyone's guess. He leans to the bars, rubs his chin. "So, the fuckin' thief. What did he say when he got his wish? When he met you?"

I stare up at him, deadpan. More tired than I've ever been.

Thief? Is this real?

"Oh, come now, Alice," he says, and reaches his fingers through the bars, caressing my cheek. I don't refuse him. "Here, you answer me, and I'll remind *you*. Hell, what's it matter now anyway, fuck it."

I glare at him, too weak for much else. My bones are molten hot, though even the pain has become numb, stale.

"Help me help you, girl. Tell me."

Hannah Grace flashes through my mind. A once-pulsing heart deflates in my fist.

I clear my raw throat. "He said that he birthed the world and everyone in it. He was insane, in another reality…"

"The bastard injected it, didn't he…" He shakes his head, chuckling, scratching the scruff of his cheeks. "Hell, I wouldn't have even sent you if I'd known that…but he was right, in a way. See, we each have our own universe, Alice. The world is nothing more than intersecting realities." He points to his head. "We call them lives; bit easier to manage that way."

A wide sky full of stars. Just outside Richmond, Virginia. Bodachi tips back his PBR, wipes the beer from his then beard, and looks to me. We're seated on top of the big rig for the very first time, years ago now. I give him a chance because Hannah trusts him, though deep down I imagine whatever he's convinced her of is no more than farfetched hearsay. She said she'd had a surprise for me. That she'd gotten in with certain hushed circles of the Richmond underground, all while I debauched my nights away since arriving in Poe Country.

"So," he says, a few beers in now. "Time to stump the immortal." He turns to me, burps. "Alice, is it?"

I smirk, nod. "Alice Ann, but I'll allow it."

"How can you trust what you perceive, Alice Ann?" He's drunk, though I'm not naive. I know it's intentional, his vulnerability with me a sign of good faith, trust, and so I decide to hear him out. "All you see from behind those two holes in your skull?" He leans back with a groan, grabs another can from the cooler behind him, and snaps the tab. It hisses. "The only one you can vouch for is yourself." He pulls down his lids, shows the pink flesh beneath. "You can't crawl into my head, experience the world as I see it, if I see it at all. You'll never know if anyone's truly here but yourself, so why act so sure?"

I smirk. "Is this your way of an introduction? Drunk philosophizing?"

He pulls from his beer and tips up his trucker hat, staring off at the Richmond skyline. "Hmph, that's what I thought. You and all your vast years avoiding the question..."

Despite myself, I like this one. He's bold, unafraid, though Hannah says he works with our kind often, but I wasn't listening all that much. I don't put stock into pipe dreams, rumors.

"I trust my senses," I reply, and scan the city

lights as well. *"I hear your heart beating, right now, calm and slow, like a dying man."*

"But don't all dreams feel real?" He winks and turns his gaze to the crunching of gravel and leaves behind us, to Hannah Grace walking up the path. *Her eyes are dome lights in the distance, like a cat's. She lifts her hand, waves. "You'll both be taken care of,"* he continues, sips his beer. *"Your sister has seen to that."* He lifts it to me, a toast of sorts. *"Time to see the world, girl."*

I open my eyes to the trailer's interior, to Bodachi looking down on me. "Figured I'd wait till you came to." He sighs, rolls his neck. "I *know* you *know*, girl. Haven't worked out the *how*, but it doesn't matter. Truth is, you've seen us before, Hannah Grace and me. She's made you forget a few times."

My stomach plummets. *How long has this been going on?* And yet, hope dawns. *Why do all this, tell me everything, if not to make me forget? They probably have Imani in Bodachi's trailer, giving her the same treatment. She must be so damned scared.*

I wish I hadn't fed her the dreamer's blood now, hadn't inoculated her so that she might have a chance at forgetting all this.

"I don't know what you've thought this whole time, but the Wranglers, well, we're not a charity case. We don't cart you around out of the *goodness of our spotless souls*. Hannah knew, but also knew you wouldn't approve. *'Too headstrong,'* she said,

67 | SCOTT J. MOSES

and so the only stipulation to our agreement was that you couldn't know. Naturally, I agreed."

He chuckles. "But you," he wags his finger at me, "You were always *so damn difficult*. You don't know how many times I almost left you high and dry while you were out on your *excursions*, picking off drunks, clubbing, or at seedy speakeasies or whatever it is you do. So many times, Alice. So many. But Hannah, well—even if she'd just given blood and was too weak to stand—would *beg* me to wait. Beg me not to leave you stranded." He chuckles. "She'd even threaten to stay herself, but when that didn't work, as she knew it wouldn't, she'd sit right back down and roll up her sleeve. Give a bit more. Another fifteen minutes. A half hour. An hour, sometimes, in hopes you'd show up before she passed out, or worse. I know, strange, right? That your kind needs blood in your veins like us. I wouldn't have ever believed that was the case if I hadn't seen it myself."

If I was low, I'm lower now. All that recklessness. Exploring the world, all those nights Hannah Grace stayed back when I went out on the proverbial town. She gave herself for me, *actually bled* for me. Who knows how many times she's done so...so many...so so many. I wasn't hurting Bodachi, or myself, staying out much later than allotted, ignoring their rules, but her, Hannah Grace, the only one I have in this world. And maybe, deep down, I knew that. I mean, the memories were there, right? I only had to remember... We can charm ourselves; I see that now. We convince ourselves of just about anything to feel on top of it all. Comfortable, safe, more than…

My eyes well with tears, but I won't cry. Not here. Not now.

"Ah, hell," he says, and something like sympathy drowns his features. "You think I *enjoy* this? Because I don't, girl. I don't. Hell, I'd like to be on a beach somewhere, far off from all this shit with my little girl." It's he who wipes his eyes now. I've never seen him cry before. He removes a leather billfold, akin to the dreamer's, from his back pocket. "I dream of it, you know? How she'll look off to the ocean, actually *see* it one day. How she'll walk with the sand between her toes without my guidance, or the doctors', the surgeons." He opens the billfold, shakes it at me. Three crimson-filled vials. "But miracles cost money…and until then, I have bills like any other. And like Charon needs his coin to ferry the dead across Styx, so I need your blood. It's transactional, always has been. See, I got family too. And I don't take them for granted like you. That's the only reason I'm here right now. Why I'm starving you in the back of this god damned trailer with that unhinged pill-popper outside. Because I love my girl more than you love your sister. More than—"

"Hey Bodachi," Raeger says, hefting himself up into the trailer, boots thudding on the aluminum floor. He holds a satellite phone, his hand pressed over the receiver. "Call for you, from friends in high places."

A bird takes flight from one of the many branches on the small sliver of horizon.

"In a minute," Bodachi says, his teeth clenched. "I made a promise."

Raeger lowers the phone, more serious than I've seen him thus far. "It's *Big Pharma*. Get the goddamn phone."

Bodachi's eyes linger on mine a moment, another, yet another, but he growls, rises. His footfalls echoing throughout the manufactured void.

My body racks with newfound pain and I constrict, growling there, hunched in on myself. When it subsides, I manage to roll on my back, wary I'll wake it again. Grimacing with anticipation, knowing I deserve it. All the pain there is in this world. Thinking of all the times I complained of being stuck somewhere too long, as if all that time in Virginia was long at all for someone like me. How I wanted to see the world, but we could only steal so many cars without getting noticed, especially while dodging God's golden eye. And so, she goes and does this…for me. She wanted to see the world too, yes, but I think…I think it was more for baby Alice. Perhaps older siblings are like that, when no mother figure is around. Pain truly is the price of love.

I stare at the ceiling of my cage, the weight of all my sins bearing down on my chest. *Make me forget, Hannah. But I'll remember this, all of it, and over time I'll convince you you don't have to do this anymore. Won't even kill them if it means you, me, and Imani leave all this behind one day. I can be patient, can wait, but in the meantime, I'll be better to you. I'll try my damndest to be the family you deserve.*

I exhale at the sound of approaching boots, and wincing, I sit myself upright, my back against the bars. Bodachi crosses his arms, a look I can't decipher on his face.

I open my mouth to speak, and my jaw bones creak beneath my ears. I've never been without blood for this long.

"I need to talk with her. You can be there if you like, but I need to hear it from *her*. All of it. I need to know…"

He sighs, looks as if he's thinking behind those eyes. Considering. He looks away, crouches, and his eyes find mine.

"Can't happen, girl," he says, holding my gaze.

"Bodachi, *please*, I—"

He smirks, but it's small. "Alice Ann says *please*. Well, I'll be damned…" The smirk evaporates. "You *really* don't remember, do you? She's gone, Alice. They both are…"

My eyes widen, fists clench. "What do you mean, *gone*? What the hell have you done? I swear, I'll—"

Tears fill his eyes, and he wipes them away with his forearm. "*You* killed her. You killed them both."

And as he speaks, something loosens in my mind. I remember in blurred flashes. That which I was made to forget…

The black sky filled with stars.

Imani behind me as we walk up the road to the motel. Welcome Inn *in buzzing green bulbs, of which a few are dead or dying. She hasn't said a word since we left the basement, and I'm not sure whether euphoria or despair is to blame.*

And there he *is. Bodachi, talking with another wrangler who looks down on him from the driver's seat of his rig. The headlights piercing in this nowhere Virginian landscape. I've seen this one a handful of times before. We've met on deserted stretches of interstate, parkways long gone from it all, though now, I know why, what for.*

Bodachi lifts a hand to me, smiles, and I see it die when Imani walks up from behind me. He looks back into the open driver's door, and the wrangler bends below the windshield. He exits with a machete, and Bodachi holds a hand to him. I read his lips. "Whoa, whoa. Wait.*" They walk towards us.*

My gut says to stand in front of Imani, to keep what I know a secret. That I should be tactful here, learn more over time. Though my rage hasn't time for that.

I'm screaming, stomping towards him. Waving the emptied vial in the air. If there are other wrangler tenants, they remain hidden in their rooms or trucks. The buzzing neon stirs me on. The sound of uncertainty, of the unknown, cackling behind me, but not for long.

Bodachi advances, withdrawing the revolver from the small of his back. He must forget what I am, the fool. He wafts the piece in Imani's direction, I hear her stop dead behind me. "And who the hell is this, Alice? You know better than to bring someone here. You know we have rul—"

I toss the vial at his boots, growl the words. "What the hell are you and Hannah up to?"

He freezes, looks the way he did in the motel room. Pale, fish belly white, though whether from the accusation or the headlights bathing us all, I'm not sure. He pulls the hammer back on his revolver, looks over his shoulder, and screams. "Han—" But he stops short. She's already there, already walking past the wranglers, hands up as if warming herself over a fire, calming a rabid beast. The fingers of my right hand twitch for war.

"Alice," she says, slowing her pace. "Sister, love, you need to forget, okay? Forget."

I'm caught in her gaze, because that's how we talk, direct eye contact and with nothing to hide, or so I thought. And though I can't look away, I'm still advancing, though slower now. Something in my mind awakened, fortified.

My claws grow long as I point to the vial. Bodachi lifts his revolver from behind her. He's shaking. The other wrangler grips his machete, unwavering. His eyes are dead, glazed, as if he's on something.

"What the hell is happening, Hannah?" My eyes on Bodachi now, in case he runs. "Tell me."

A docile footstep in the gravel behind me.

I whip around. My hand extending as if to protect my young. Someone in the shotgun seat as the car comes head on. "Stay behind me!" I call to Imani, hear her stop dead.

"I thought you said it was safe?" she asks. "Your home...?"

"Yeah," I say, turning back to Hannah, all of them. "I thought so."

Hannah's closer now, her eyes widening. "Alice," she says, and her voice shakes. "I love you. I always have, always will. I can explain everything. I can, really, *but you* have *to calm down. You have to—"*

"I'll hear it all," I say, trudging towards Bodachi, who steps back with my advance. "After he's torn in two."

She blocks my path, though we're still a few yards from one another. The night's quiet overhead, no wind to speak of. The only town for miles the one I just left. Only us in this nowhere motel parking lot, forgotten by many and all. Owned and operated by wranglers.

Who are they...?

"Alice, listen to me." Blood runs from her eyes to the gravel at her feet. "Please. We have a good thing here. Just, stop.*" Her eyes widen, and I feel my body give way. As if I walk against a torrential wind. "You have to STOP," she says again, and though I'm slow, drowsy—I'm still coming. She throws a look over her shoulder to Bodachi—who*

looks terrified—back to me. "Stop, Alice! Stop! Please, please, you have to stop!" Her eyes so wide. The veins in her face, red and bulging.

She jerks as if shot, though no weapon was fired, and my body crumples. I slam face-first into the ground, though I don't feel it. My body in a stalemate with itself, akin to sleep paralysis. Watching the nightmare of my sister convulsing on the ground—blood running from her startled eyes, her lips, nose now. Her mouth opens... closes... opens... closes. Her blood-filled eyes gleaming in the night. It's muffled, but Bodachi screams her name. Bridging the gap between them in a fervor. He collapses and gathers her into his arms, cradling her twitching, slack form. And even as the wrangler walks past me, machete in hand, I can't break Hannah's gaze, the motion of her barely parting lips. Their pattern. She's trying to say something to me, but I can't make the words for all the blood. Bodachi cries to the sky, rocking her back and forth. It reminds me of Pa. Bodachi always said we were like daughters, but it's only now I truly believe.

Hannah Grace, though weak, lifts her head to me, and I hear her whisper atop Bodachi's sobs. "Sleep," she says, the sound a maelstrom in my mind. "Forget..."

And as her head lolls, I can't even cry from the paralysis. My vision blurs at the periphery, a thinning tunnel. Something's lobbed from behind me, and it rolls into my dissipating view. I meet its *brown eyes. Imani's severed head. Her mouth ajar, as if shy, and about to speak. I wait for her words as blood pools around the torn skin of what's left of her throat. Darkness takes me.*

I wake, or at least it seems that way, and Bodachi's still crouched beyond the bars, watching me. Tears line his lids, though his lips remain taut.

I'm crying now, can't hold it in anymore. The blood falling to the floor in a volley of *taps*.

"You and Hannah," he says, clearing his throat. "You're the only ones I've ever seen cry. And only for one another."

I force my head into my knees, my arms wrapped around my entirety. My groans that of a damned beast.

I hear him rise through my wails. "We're each dealt our own unique affliction, Alice. Ours is death. Yours? Yours is life."

His footfalls recede, vibrating the aluminum floor, and through burning vision I watch him go. He stops, and glances over his shoulder. "I'm sorry, girl. I loved her too."

The sun envelops his form in what space the doors allow. How its light seeps into the dark, clawing its way in at me. How I long for it to reach me now. Knowing Bodachi nor Raeger know what they truly do. *Sun poisoning.* They think if they dangle death before me I'll tremble, like perhaps many have in the past. But I'm as those deserted sailors, shipwrecked on some forsaken cough of land, bleached and boiling, dying of thirst while looking out on all that beckoning salt water. They know it's bad, and so most refrain though tempted, all while others with the same knowledge know the water is ultimately *good*. That it will set them free from all of it. *Everything*.

My fists slam the trailer floor. My grief a second wind of strength. And as exhaustion takes me, my bones and body comprised of lead again, the sunlight narrows as he shuts the doors, leaves me there in the dark.

I'm falling, or am I? What is this? *This is starvation, Alice. Me talking to you, who is me. The you who thinks within you.*

Where am I falling from? *When did we begin to end?* Where am I going? *And when did we end to end...?*

"Alice Ann, are you paying attention?"

I'm bound in the corner of the room where Ma schooled us. I can't move. My arms pulled behind me in a straitjacket. The room's all wood: wooden floors, wooden walls, wooden desks. A single window separates the space into two make-shift sections. It's night through the glass.

"Alice?"

"Yes, Ma. I'm listening."

Hannah Grace is in the corner adjacent to me in a straitjacket as well, chained to the floor. She struggles, pulling against her restraints until they *clink*, grow taut.

Ma sets her chalk down on the blackboard's base, closes her Bible, eyeing us each in turn. "I don't know what's gotten into you two tonight, but seeing as you're more than like elsewhere in heads or minds or wherever young girls drift off to, I want you to listen now, hear?" She sighs, rises, and I hear it now, echoing in my skull. The *lub-lub* of her heart. The artery beneath her jawbone. She lifts her hair with thin fingers, grey mixed with brown. "Every grey hair, children, is a reminder God's comin'—He and His angel, Death—but it's not something to be feared. Everything fades, girls. Everything."

Hannah's snarling now, and before I know it, I'm up as well. Standing, writhing in my chains, yanking at them with my entirety. Feeling the cheap, dilapidated boards giving bit by bit around me. Hannah's chains straining, hairline cracks webbing the wall behind. Drool runs in lines from her lips to the floor, *our* lips. I only hear my mother's heartbeat. *So hungry...*

Ma walks towards me now, Bible in hand, and as she gets closer, I scream in my mind for her to stop, but I don't have control anymore. My mouth hangs open, deep growl in my throat. Saliva runs along my fangs and tongue. If Ma notices, she doesn't let on.

She kneels before me. "Let's pray, Alice." She clasps her hands, and I'm inches from her, yanking at my binds, tearing at the chains in the wall, snarling like some animal, no—the thing I am. I see red, the *pulse pulse* of her heart excruciating as the thumping bass of every venue I've frequented.

"Now, girls," she says, eyes peeling open again, the Bible in her lap. "There are many great lessons in this book, and frankly, I could go on for the rest of my life about them. Trying to instill in you both the values which were taught to your Pa and I." She sighs, sets the tome down beside her, stares into my eyes. "We are all born on a pulpit, Alice. Our lives are the only sermons that matter." I jerk forward as the chains give, and as I dive at her, Hannah Grace looms in the air above me—just two hungry girls looking to their mother for sustenance.

In the void again, *falling*. This is what my life is like, if it can be called one at all.

What's that, Alice? What's that, me?

Well, it's strange to say.

Come on, it's just us now.

Well, sometimes I feel I'll slip right through the floor.

We long for warmth, though we've forgotten its meaning, that it?

Well, yes, but not only that. The worst part is that I couldn't tell you, me, when it ceased to be real for us at all.

I can.

Yeah?

Yeah.

Well, enlighten me.

Warmth itself died long ago, but the promise of warmth? That died with Hannah. And the hope that you could do anything but be cruel in this world? With the astronomer, the newborn, Imani.

The gravel bites into my cheek. Bodachi's wails hot and distorted upon the ether. Hands gently lower Imani's severed head in my view. Raeger positions her upright, as not to fall, and brushes the hair from her eyes, tucks it behind an ear. Imani stares at me, blinks, and her mouth creeps open. "You envy me," she says, blinks again. "Even more than when I was alive."

The dust in my mouth, gravel gnawing my skin. "I'm sorry. I never meant—"

"You could've sat anywhere in that cafe," she continues. "Why not beside the old man at the bar's end? Any one of those vacant tables?"

"I needed the storefront, a view of the street."

She scrunches her lips, like I'm a child who's shown their mother their terrible art. "But no, you chose the closest thing to you. The you you're not and will never be again. Corrupted it, like plucking a flower…."

I'm willing myself to move, to look over and around her, screaming in my mind for Hannah to make me forget this, all of it. Just to catch a glimpse before she dies so she can—even now, after everything, I'm using her. Is that a *smile* on Imani's lips?

And as her mouth creeps open again, she mouths familiar words to me. "*Stay too close to the living and you'll swallow them up."*

Plummeting now. Down down down…

The Baltimorean skyline spreads out before us as the rig punctures the city limits. The white and purple light luminescent from the stadium in the sky full of stars.

Wait, I know this…

Do you? Do we?

This is a memory, or at least, I think it is.

Hannah's on the bed in the cabin behind us. I'm riding shotgun. The manufactured northern lights ushering us in as we pull onto the main drag. The harbor and its glistening, black water to our right.

Bodachi chuckles, tapping the wheel to the tune of Marlon Williams' "Dark Child". "So, you're telling me you can drink *whatever* you want, but you can't taste any of it?"

Hannah shifts behind us. "That's right. Most places you all go require one to sit with a beverage, or to at least palm one for a while."

"And your bodies, what, just burn up the liquid? Is that it?"

I sigh, swiveling my gaze from a docked ship to him. "All we know is that drink is fine, but food…doesn't go over so well."

The brakes hiss as we pull to a stop at the newly red traffic light. He turns to us. "Why's that, I wonder?" he asks. The downtown streets filled with headlights. Swarms of pedestrians on the side and crosswalks swept in the hustle of their lives.

"Hell, we don't know," Hannah says. "This is all

trial and error."

"So why do you both drink whiskey then? I mean, don't get me wrong, my drink of choice as well, but why so specific if you can't even taste it?"

Hannah doesn't miss a beat. "Our pa drank whiskey."

The truck is silent a moment, and I wonder if this conversation has run its course, but Bodachi drums the wheel again, and Hannah Grace laughs in that breathy way through her nose. We're blowing his mind right now.

He jolts from a horn's bellow behind us, stalling at the green light a second too many for these Baltimoreans. We lurch forward. "How about running water? Can you cross it?"

Hannah from behind us. "We went over a bridge five minutes ago and didn't explode in your truck, so there's that."

He holds a hand up, embarrassed smile on his face. "All right, okay, hold on now, how about being invited in? My grandmother—long before I got into all this—wouldn't have welcome mats at her door for fear of inviting something in."

Hannah smirks in the rearview mirror. "As if we ever *needed* inviting."

My eyes dart to Hannah's reflection, back to Bodachi. "We go where we like."

Memories in shuttered flashes.

I'm a child, in town with Pa to get supplies for the farm. It's sweltering, and as we traverse the sparse wood and brick buildings, the wind does little to cool us.

A pair of men unload a wagon a 'ways up the road, each clenching the handle of a metal milk drum, and as they bare their teeth, the container unsteadies in their hands. A part of me waits for the spill. The ruin where everything crumbles. And for the first time, I realize I'm what's wrong with the world."

In a city, long ago, but what's long for someone like me? I pull the knife from my chest as the mugger steps backward, shocked with dreadful wonder. I drop it to the ground, sizing up the starved man, his leather jacket. He steps back and I catch his eyes. He slackens, drooping perhaps from withdrawal, my mind, or both. I scan the alley for something creative, a way to pull wings from this fly. The worn bricks of the warehouse speak to me. "Slide your cheek along the wall," I say with a smile, hardly containing myself. "Till the bone shows."

He goes to do so, and I jerk. "Wait." He does. "Give me your jacket." I've always liked leather.

Selfish.

Yes.

Narcissist.

Yes.

"You know," Bodachi says, as we cross a bridge over the ocean headed to Norfolk. These were the early days, perhaps weeks into pairing with the wranglers. "I've been thinking."

My face, deadpan. "Have you now?"

"So, there's the world that exists independently

of ourselves, and there's how we perceive that world, yeah?" Boats crawl below us over the black, churning waters. Ocean for as long as I can see in that fogged night. Bodachi lifts a hand from the steering wheel, empty beer cans rattle at his feet near the pedals. *Of course...*

He points to his head. "Ever heard of the Phaneron?" He shrugs his shoulders, actually hiccups. "Hell, maybe the sky's really green, but we *perceive* blue." I mean, dogs see it all in black and white, yeah? Could you tell a dog the sky was blue and actually *know* it to be true?"

"That's a myth."

"What is?"

"That dogs see in black and white. They see some yellows, blues too."

"Where'd you learn something like that?"

"Hannah told me."

He sighs. "Well, if *Hannah* says so it's obviously true."

I smirk. "Well then, smartass, that fact aside, dogs can't speak now, can they? So, it's irrelevant."

He smiles in a way I've not seen before, and thumbs the photo attached via fishing hook to his sun-visor. A picture of an old and greying mutt. Next to it is another of a woman and little girl at the beach. The image leans a bit, as if the photographer had a few too many PBRs. "Oh, but they can...speak, that is," he says, caressing the dog's image with his thumb. "And they do."

In a low-lit bar now, adorned in wood in every

aspect: wooden counter, stools, and paneled walls, rustic. The bartender slides me a whiskey. I nod, and as I bring it to my lips, the patrons shuffling in from the cold behind me, freeze. Mid-smile, mid-breath, mid-thought. Their hearts aren't beating, though they show no signs of distress. A familiar smell on the air...*Hannah.*

I turn in my stool to the dreamer who sits atop a table, his feet on the bench between two sheep mid-conversation. In one hand, he holds a martini—olive and everything—in the other, he cradles his intestines and what I think is his liver. He smiles and sips his drink. If he's in pain, it doesn't show.

"If you think about it," he says, blood and bile seeping through the gaps between his fingers. "I'm right."

I sip my whiskey. "Oh yeah?"

He lifts himself onto the table now, lets the hand holding his innards fall away. They spill out and onto the table, bench, and those seated there, they and their frozen smiles.

"Compared with how long we don't exist—the time prior to birth and that after death," he arches himself backward, looks to the ceiling. "This life really *is* just some dream, you know? A blink in the immense gap of it all. A dash between dates on each of our tombstones."

He thinks he's clever.

"*You* never got a tombstone," I say with a smile.

He bends forward, hunching over, and lifts his glass to something behind me. "Neither did *she.*"

I turn to the stench of smoke searing my nostrils, to Hannah Grace in our old bedroom. I'm laying there, covers up to my eyes, watching her up in flames. She slides off her bed, stepping over our slain parents, and crawls into mine with me. And though the flames roar, they don't catch my bed, sheets, or me ablaze, but her skin—it's peeling, crusted-black, and cracking as she spoons me.

"How are you, Alice?" she asks, and it's all I can do to hear her over the flames. She runs her fingers over the puncture marks in my throat. "How do you *feel*?"

"I can't," I say into the blanket. "I *don't*..." Never once thinking to ask how *she* was. She'd always held *me*, and in over two lifetimes, I'd rarely returned the favor.

We no longer feel her imprint on the earth.

Who are we? *We don't know.*

Where do we come from? *Who knows?*

Where are we going? *There.*

How long do we have to get *there*? *Forever, but what's* really *forever...?*

I'm seated on the curb behind a New England club, crying into my hands. "I'm so sorry, Hannah. I'm—"

"Everything, okay?"

It's her, *Julia*, looking down on me. And though her mascara's in lines, she smiles, her iPhone in hand. Rain mists the air, hangs there in wait. I open my mouth to speak.

"You haven't called," she says, and lifts the

phone to her ear as if reminding me how. I bite my lip, and can't bring myself to tell her, though the thought's on my tongue. That if I don't call, the possibility of something going right is still available, floating out there on the ether somewhere. Who am I to dispel that chance, to kill it, like everything else I touch? If I leave it be, I won't have to find out how it all doesn't work out.

"It's so sad," she says, sitting next to me on the curb. "That it takes losing someone to realize what they meant to you."

I'm awake, *awake* awake, tears running down my cheeks. The aluminum floor is cool on my skin. The rig's doors are open wide, allowing the night in. I dig around in my jacket—my burner long gone—retrieving the receipt with Julia's lipstick-scrawled number, and though I'm lost in the dark from starvation, my vision not what it used to be, I take it in. I lick my still falling tears, and the blood tastes *good*.

Replacing the number, I withdraw an arm from my jacket, and rolling the hoodie's sleeve up, my teeth break the skin. The notion's never dawned on me to feed from myself, though I haven't starved like this before. I think of Bodachi and Raeger. How they must have plans for me, having kept me alive this long, and how that's fine. I deserve whatever hell comes my way. I drink in deep and my eyes roll back, but when nausea takes hold, I withdraw. The night's brighter now. Rolling down my sleeve, I slide my arm back into my jacket, prop myself against the bars. Come what may, but if this is prison, how it all ends as it should for me—I want my phone call.

CHAPTER 4
RELIEF AND OTHER LIES

I jar from sleep to a maelstrom of metal biting metal, and backing to the rearmost bars of my cage, my wits find me. Raeger's sliding a machete along the bars, *back* and *forth*, *baaaack* and *foooorth*. The reverberation echoes throughout the all but empty trailer, some gargantuan locomotive from hell.

He steps back, smirks. "Looks like someone's been crying. Why so sad?" He examines the blade as if curious, rubbing his thumb over a discolored blemish in the otherwise pristine metal. A tinge of brownish-red, Imani's blood.

The hooks of my mind quake, tremble for use, but I refuse them. Have to be wise here, though I'm not trying to escape. Not anymore, I've been escaping my whole life; time to meet something head on for a change. I find his eyes, that smirk.

"You're all *filth*," he says, pointing the machete my way.

Boots pound aluminum. "That's enough, Raeger," Bodachi says, calm, but stern, his ham fists all but clenched at his sides.

He stops before the bars, between Raeger and I. Raeger scoffs and posts up against the trailer wall, shaking his head in disapproval.

The dam behind my eyes threatens to break, but I hold fast. "Why didn't she tell me, Bodachi? Why keep it from me?"

"Your sister," he begins, clearing his throat as if holding something back as well, "she was smart. She knew you'd react...the way you did. She knew you best, and so I trusted her lead, so long as she provided what we agreed upon."

I should've left it alone...but how could I?

"What happens now?"

"I think you know, Alice. What do *you* think?"

Cool wind rolls in through the trailer entrance. The darkness breathing life into this three-fourths room.

"I wager you'll take my blood, get your supply from the only one still available to you. Someone who won't resist... I'm done fighting, Bodachi. I'm done with most things now..."

He smiles like a father correcting a child who's said some absurdity. "You act as if you're valuable because of what you are. There are others more than willing to give blood for a free roaming existence." Raeger chuckles from behind him, and Bodachi flings a look over his shoulder. Raeger stills, smiles. "You're not like Hannah," Bodachi continues. "Amiable. Respectable. Eager to cooperate. You know, we'd talk when you were out on your escapades, whether giving blood or not. We'd talk on all sorts of things." He leans in, and if I could meld into the bars behind me I would. "She'd tell me that she never really felt *there*, present. Like she might evaporate at any moment. How she sometimes longed for it, but knew she had to be there for her baby sister. That that was why she existed. As far as she was concerned, she'd died long ago, was your living angel. Your guardian, no more, no less."

The dam finally breaks, and I grit my teeth, jerk up at him. "You're *lying*."

He sighs. "What reason do I have to lie, girl? Tell me."

I don't have an answer.

Raeger zips up his bomber jacket, sheathes the machete, and unholsters his revolver. He spins the wheel, and satisfied, locks it into place. Bodachi extends his hand back to him, his eyes still on mine, and Raeger bends to the military duffel at his feet, removes something I don't quite catch, holds it forward. Bodachi accepts, and pushes it through the bars, it sails to the floor at my feet. An emptied burlap of animal feed, like the ones I used to rest my head on in the early days, when all was well, or seemed to be.

"Put that on, girl," he says, and removes a ring of keys from his pocket, picking through them. "Go on," he repeats, and I do so. Obscurity envelops my world. "And best stop your crying. We've a walk yet."

The door clicks, and after a pause, iron moans.

I shift my gaze to where he was, might still be. The scent of barley and corn smothering my senses.

"Before whatever this is happens, I need to make a call. Do what you will, but you promise me my call, Bodachi. *Promise me.*"

A long exhale. Handcuffs fasten to my wrists, bite in tight. "The only real gods in this world are uncertainty and death. You might get your call, you might not. We'll just have to see. Though you for *sure* worship death. I've seen you since you've been with us, longing for it like a cure…so, consider me its prophet, lighting the way for you."

I go my own way. The thought is automatic. That rebellious remnant of myself not yet quelled.

"Come on, Alice," he says. "Let's get this done."

My hands feel for the bars, and finding them, I pull myself into the world again. Fucked thing is, I miss the cage.

Bodachi's boots pound the aluminum floor, receding toward the entrance. I pause, unsure of my footing.

"Go on," Raeger says, and cocks the hammer as if I need coaxing. "I've been *waiting* for this. Think you have too." Blind, I walk, thankful for the blood leached from myself, for the ability to stand, to do one last thing with dignity.

Sticks, rocks, and all else crunch beneath our boots as we trudge through the forest. The terrain at an incline as we go. Leaves rustle above us as if hushing each other for some new doom. The wind's an exhale in our faces, has been the entire time, though I can't estimate time. How long we've been walking. Could've been an age, could've been ten minutes.

Raeger presses the revolver to my back. "Get moving. You wanna *see*, right?"

Footsteps ahead of me pause, the sound of someone pivoting. "We've plenty of time. She'll see it." They start up crunching nature again. So do I.

The blood I bled has given me means to walk, but it's a haze. As if I've a foot in reality and the other still in the oblivion I'd begun to make a home. Teetering there, longing for a decisive gust to blow me this way or that. My bones ache, and each step sends a tremor through me reminiscent of the pangs I had upon waking behind bars. That bit of blood won't sustain me much longer. Birdsong, placating and jovial, springs up here and there, and I glance to the scattered cries, trying to pin down each orator. Remember what Pa used to say: *that dawn comes with birdsong.*

"Raeger," Bodachi says further up. "Ease off her. We're fine."

As the barrel leaves my back, Raeger mutters under his breath. "*Fuck you. We're using* my *truck,* my *gear...*"

I lose the rest to the birds again, bathing in their chorus, though I know I don't deserve it.

Bodachi's footfalls shift direction and I home in on them like a blind hound, my nose upturned. The night's scents meld with something *other* now, something I've not smelled in a long while, but can't place.

Dawn, or at least its approach. Can't be far off now.

Bodachi exhales, boots crunching nature's detritus as he approaches. "We're here, girl."

As the sack's ripped from my face, I take a moment to gather myself. I'm on a mountain. The cliff's edge marked by a crude wooden barrier not far from us, overlooking a sprawling valley rife with pines. A river snaking through their needling masses. Behind me, a tunnel of stone vomits train tracks up the mountain a 'ways barred by a steep brush-ridden crag. The wind howls.

"I'll admit, girl," Bodachi says, leaning against a fallen tree. I thought you'd have passed by now." Raeger cups a hand around his lighter to my other side, cigarette dangling from his lips. He sits upon a makeshift bench just shy of the overlook. He shakes his head. Bodachi continues, "I figured you'd earned this, though I would've brought you here to burn eventually regardless."

The dirt at my boots is more ash than soil, spreading all the way to where cliff meets open air. Strewn about and in patches nearest the cliff's edge, no less blown by an indecisive wind. I fall to my knees, group a handful between my cupped hands, peering into it, into *them*.

Tell me, Imani says in my mind. *How many dead stars am I made of?*

Hannah is silent.

I'd cry, but my grief is beyond tears now. A heaviness compounding gravity. *Let this be the end...*

Shaking, I lift their remains to my face. "I'm so sorry," I say, my face closer now. "I'm so so sorry..."

Bodachi wipes his eyes with a forearm. "You know I think of you as a daughter, right?"

I stare off the overpass, train my gaze on twin headlights winding their way through the lonely dirt road I'd missed.

Raeger chuckles, draws from his cigarette. "You're too close, Bodachi." He taps the ashes from its end. "You've gotten soft."

"Watch it, Raeger."

"*No*, no," he continues, rising from the bench now. He points to me. "You see that? *That* right *there* ain't no *girl*." He stands before me now, looking me in the eye—close, too close. "Might *look* like a girl. Might *talk* like one, hell, might even breathe on occasion—" He turns to Bodachi, showing me his back. "But it ain't. And you best learn that with the next haul you recruit. They'll turn on you first chance they get, that's why I have that cage in the back of my rig, because I have *boundaries*, because I'm in *charge*."

Bodachi repositions himself against the tree now. "Let her mourn, Raeger. Sun's coming soon enough. Just let it be. Show some respect."

Raeger wags his finger, pivots back to me. "No

no, Bodachi. See, you're gonna get yourself killed one day, and I don't wanna think back to this moment and not have called you out on it all." He bends low to me, and I lower my ash-filled hands. "What are you?"

I lift my head, don't meet his gaze. "That which shouldn't be."

"Little louder for the asshole over there."

Bodachi looks the father now, fists clenched, and steps forward.

The ashes slip through my fingers, rejoining the whole. "A shadow's ghost…"

Raeger smirks, rises, turns back to Bodachi. "Bit extravagant for my taste. What she—*it*, means to say, is that it's nothing but manipulation and bloodlust in a skinsuit pulled taut over itself." He points back to me with his thumb. "That *ain't* no girl."

"All right, fine, *fine*…" Bodachi says. "You've made your point, but if you want me to uphold my end of our agreement, you'll stand down. Let this run its course."

Raeger chuckles, shakes his head, walking out to the overlook, and lights up another cigarette.

I slump in the ashes, lay down there, my face flush with them, tears held back by a numbness I've never known. *I'm sorry…I'm so sorry…*

Bodachi's talking, though I can't make out the words for the roaring apologies, the regrets which won't let me rest, won't let me go. *A girl in my mind then, hunched over her phone on the curb.*

Something stirs in me, and my eyes find Bodachi philosophizing on his tree as if a captive crowd sits before him.

"...I think that's the scariest part of death. There's no recounting it."

I lift my head from the ash.

"No certain after," he continues. "You experience it, but can't pass the feeling on..."

"Bodachi," I say, on a knee now.

"...And what are the living without stories?"

I stand, swaying from the exertion. "Bodachi, my call. You promised."

Raeger's eyes burn holes into me from the overlook, hand on his revolver.

"I never promised anything, girl," he says, scanning the valley below. I think he *wants* to look at me but can't.

I step towards him. "You *promised*." Raeger slips his cannon from its holster.

Bodachi sighs, steps off the tree he's been leaning on. "Can't see how that's beneficial anymore, girl. We're *here*. Let's just, I don't know...*be*."

My brows furl, my fangs sliding down my still taut lips. I take another step, and whip around, the trees a blurred maelstrom surrounding me in a fissure. The roar of Raeger's revolver echoing over the valley as I fall to the ground back first, flush with the ashes again. Eyes on the night sky.

Raised voices now. Someone standing over me in my blurred vision. The brushing whispers of the golden field, its dandelions. The donkey snorts as he trots off. Pa bends to me, smiling. *"If you're ever distraught, child, you take a look up at that sun there. That's God's eye. His love. Let that comfort you, hear?"*

"I miss you, Pa...you and Ma, Hannah—" The words choke. A constellation of faces bear down on me. Pa in his overalls. Ma in that dress worn for teachin', despite school being at the farmhouse. Imani, laptop in hand, a sternness in her gaze, and Hannah, blood in lines from her eyes, ears, and nose. That deadpan expression all but unreadable, though I see through its facade—disappointment.

One thing before I repent. Before I'm dragged off to whatever hell I deserve by those I loved and let down. Just one thing, then you can have me.

The grass dissipates, as do their faces. The wrangler's argument hot on the ether.

"She burns with the *sun*, like the others."

"Why is that so *goddamn* important to you?"

"She *needs* to see."

"She *needs to see?*' Dammit will you listen to yourself? She was *coming for you* when I shot her down. You're fucking oblivious, Bodachi."

Raeger turns to me, levels the gun at my head. "You can shoot me, Bodachi, but it'll have to be in the back. I've wasted enough time with you and your wallowing sentimentality. It's gonna get you killed, friend..."

I kiss the barrel with my forehead, and positioning it between my eyes, whisper,

"Please..."

He glances back over his shoulder to Bodachi. The robins sing in off-kilter rhythm. "See? It *wants* this. You gonna deny family what they want?"

Bodachi draws his revolver now, the click of the hammer piercing the air. "Are *you* telling me what's best for *my* family? You and those *pills* you pop like Tic Tacs, telling *me* that? Fuck you, Raeger."

"Someday, far off from now," Raeger says, his gaze sliding over me, still speaking to Bodachi. "You'll thank me for this. You'll see how she was manipulating you. How they *both* were. That's how they survive, Bodachi. Seduction."

He pulls the hammer of his revolver back. The click reverberating through my skull. "Oh, to give you my final opinion, a deduction after these days spent together, but there's no time for that." He smirks. "Ask me how you did before," he says, tilting my head back with the barrel. "*Beg* me to."

I meet his eyes, vision wavering with the effort. "Put two in his knees..."

He stumbles backward, his tongue lolling, his form slackens, pistol half-raised at his side. I widen my eyes, and though his dilate, they do so out of unison. The push isn't that hard. See, he already *wants* to. I'm just the nudge he needs.

He turns, stops, and raises his pistol. Gun fire erupts now, the birds taking flight. A bullet forces me low again. This one above knee.

A once-golden field, now bathed in that sweetest of smells. Blood falls like rain from a crimson sky, painting the roof of the distant farmhouse, the donkey, my family, Imani, Hannah Grace, the drifter, me, in a fervor of slapping hands—*red*.

Raeger twitches on his back, gasping for breath from the bullets torn through his chest and throat. A geyser spurting from the severed artery. I mount him, meet his eyes now, and unhinge my jaw as wide as it will go, feel it dangling there loose within the skin a moment, before my face and fangs plunge into his throat. I gorge on him, moaning, growling, animal in nature. *I'm elsewhere: Hannah and I vigilant from our spot in the trees, glaring down at the coyotes picking away at our slain parents. We give each other a look, and our pained stomachs urge us down. We don't run at them, no...we're on all fours, mouths wider than any mouth should be. Seeing red. They yelp, turn to flee, but they're slow, so very slow...*

I detach from him with a gasp. The once-drowned now swallowing the air. The colors of the night returning. The smells and true clarity of it all rushing back. My body forces the bullet from my knee and shoulder. It's only now I register his eyes, wide and terrified beneath me. I heave in the night out of sheer pleasure, pull the handcuffs apart like they're nothing, and gripping his cheeks like a child, lean in close. "The only way I could value your opinion more is valuing it at all."

I wrench his neck till it *pops* and digging through his bag—find what I'm searching for. I rise, smell Bodachi before I see him. He's back against that tree, holding his torso, the spreading crimson there. Raeger wasn't a bad shot, and Bodachi's left knee and thigh pool with red. He's screaming, eyes clenched. They peel open with my approach.

His first shot goes wide, missing me entirely. The second punches through my sternum, though I don't so much as budge. He pulls the trigger again, again, again, a resounding *click* with each of my steps.

"I love you, girl, *please*," he says, grimacing. The revolver falls from his hand, and he reaches for his wounded leg.

I bend to him, inches from his face. Raeger's blood still moist on my lips, chin, and tongue. "Call me *girl* again…"

He recoils, pressing himself into the rough bark of the tree, avoids my gaze.

"I witnessed the Spanish Flu kill thousands. Saw the Civil War with my own eyes, draining Union and Confederate alike. See, I'm someone, *something* that's not supposed to be here, and yet, here I *am*." I shake the orange bottle, a rattle beyond this infant's reach. "Now, *give me the goddamn phone*."

His eyes don't leave mine as he frantically searches his person, and unclipping the phone from his wet-with-blood belt, he extends it with a shaky hand. I toss the pills in his lap, linger there a while, gorging on his fear before plucking the phone from him.

I return to the ashes, the air coagulated with

birdsong, and sit where they meet the dirt. I pull the receipt from my inner pocket. *Here goes.*

I flip open Bodachi's phone, and entering the string of numbers, *pause.* The last digit's *gone.* The crumpled paper torn and charred from where the bullet entered my chest.

noNoNO...

I stare off at the horizon. *Is it brighter now?*

I opt for a 0, dial, and place it to my ear.

It *riiiings, riiiiiings...* A husky voice on the other end. *"Yeeeeelllllow."*

I hang up, try an 8 now, my eyes flicking from the screen to the horizon. With the blood has returned my true vision, though everything is brighter now, takes getting used to.

A series of digitized beeps: *"Your call cannot be completed as dialed, please hang up and—"*

I growl. The birds in their homes scream. What I'd do to hear her voice again, what I've already *done.* Bloodsucker till the end.

I redial, try 9. It *rings, riiings, riiiiiings, riiiiiiiiinnngs.*

I lower the phone, let it dangle there, and stare out over the valley. The birdsong clearer now, louder. I poise my thumb to end the call when I *hear* it: *"Hey, it's Jules. Sorry I missed you, but if you leave your name and number, I'll get back to you soon. Ciao."*

Beeeeep.

I inhale, and the breath I don't need fills my lungs. "I…" I hang up.

Well, there you go, Alice. You heard *her. The universe's held up its part of the—*

The phone buzzes in my hand. The numbers glowing from the screen. They end in 9. It vibrates *again, agaaain, agaaaaain—*

I flip it open, bring it to my ear. Silent.

Silence roars from the other end as well, until: "Hello?"

It's *her.*

Seconds of quiet pass. My throat's too tight, tongue won't work, mouth can't form the words.

An inhale through the speaker: "It's you...isn't it?"

Could mean anyone.

"Alice?"

And it's as if all weight's returned to me. Everything all at once. An outlet. I hunch over, body tensing. *No Hannah, no Imani, no one, alone, alone, alone.*

My voice chokes, and the blood runs from my eyes down my jacket, to the ashen earth. "How do you do it?" I ask. "Go on without them?" I exhale through the tears. "What's the point of a life without them in it? A life you barely held onto with both hands to begin with?"

A long pause. Static exhales in my ear. "We carry on, Alice. That's how we respect our dead."

Something Hannah said floats across my mind. *"Like how everyone walks around bitter. A coldness on the air, in their expressions—as if etched there by every wrong ever done to them. The world's cold by default, but it's warmth, selfless warmth that is the miracle."*

Tears blur my vision. My shoulders shake.

Julia inhales. "Still up for that movie?"

And despite it all, I laugh, feel her smile from the other end. My lips part to reply—I freeze. Pinks and purples have crept over the neighboring peaks. The purple losing ground to an orange red like a mad disease. Pooling over the countryside, as if someone's drawn open their curtains to let a little cosmos in.

I slam the phone shut and scramble for the crag, vaulting to the stones, climbing like never before. Slipping on the rocks and roots of the cliff-face like some runaway bride. I burst through the brush lining the side of the railroad and slip into the dark of the old tunnel. And as the sun inches in, I step back, once, twice, finally opting to climb the old, decrepit bricks. Just hanging there, just *laughing*. My bloody tears dripping to the tracks where the sun's stopped below.

Pa's voice in my head, *"That means you're alive. Means you want to stay that way."*

I drop down, walk to where the dark ends, and can't help but smile at the donkey bellowing in my mind. I look to Hannah's ashes. "His name was Klaus. Our donkey's name was Klaus."

CHAPTER 5
SUN'S STARE

It's as if I've stepped into a time machine, and twisting in my barstool, I take it all in. The low-lit bar. The globular lights hovering about the place in that *speak-easy* way. Everyone in suits and long dresses, their hair done up in the old way. 40's jazz roaring rampant from the speakers. The bartender, a heavyset man in a fedora, suit vest, and suspenders, black gauges in his ears, and boasting a throat tattoo of a dragon, places a whiskey before me. I nod in thanks.

He slides his fingers along the hat's rim, leans on the counter. "You know **Classic Monsters** was last weekend's theme, yeah?" He points over his shoulder to the flier stuck to a paint-chipped pillar. A man and woman dressed to the 9's, pistols in both their hands. It reads: **Step into the Noir.** He smiles, pours a shot for himself. "Gotta say though: the bullet holes in the jacket? The fake blood, dirt, and grime?" he raises the glass to me. "You make one hell of a zombie punk. That what we're going for here?"

I lift my whiskey to him. "Nailed it."

We turn our drinks back, and he full body shakes like a wet dog. Two young men in suits, college-age and hands clasped in one another's, take up stools not far from me. The barman moves to meet them with a smile.

The bar's a buzz with dancing couples and jazz, and I'm taken back to the 40s in Baltimore, to that dingy club where the whiskey flowed like water. I remember being transfixed by the drummer—full and sweaty, pained look on his face—as he *rat a tat tatted* the snare like his ma's life depended on it. Hannah at my side, those eyes wide and overwhelmed as well. She turns to look at me, and—no one's there. Just an empty stool between me and the men seated a seat or two over.

I turn back the whiskey again, and with every sip I think of her. That calm demeanor, the antithesis of myself, and how she's just...*gone.* How I'm still *here*, just looking for a reason to *be*—but isn't everyone? Perhaps reasons to stay aren't just handed out. Maybe you find them as you go, if your eyes are open, whether you're looking or not.

The noir boys next to me share a kiss as a big frat-type slides a bucket of beers from the bar. He nudges into my shoulder, ignorant and clearly drunk, and scoffs, mutters something I and the couple both hear. He puffs out his chest, as if to continue, but refrains when a roaring cheer climbs over the general noise of the crowd. He lifts the beers to the sky, and heads back to his *bros* he so lovingly refers to.

One of the men slumps at the bar, crying as his partner consoles him, all while flashing angry looks back at the mouth-breather's table. I read their lips:

Wanna go? the one in the fedora asks, casting a glance back at the loudening horde, oblivious and pulling from their beers. Shouting at any and all who walk through the sticker-plastered front door.

As the tender passes me, I wave him down, pointing to the whiskey still on the bar. I flash four fingers, nudging my chin to the couple, who are pulling on their coats, pushing in their stools. The barman nods and lines up four shot glasses, pouring whiskey into each. He slides me mine, and walks two over to the young men, who pause, confused as he hands them theirs. He points at me, and I lift my glass to them all. We shoot them back, and I tap the bar with the glass's bottom. The bartender follows suit.

I think the jury's still out on what that actually means, though I've heard all manner of things. That it's done in respect for all the unseen members of the bar: the cooks, bar backs, tenders, servers, etc. I've heard that it's to dispel spirits in the liquor itself, and that in not doing so after consumption is a provocation. A bad omen. Most believe it's a toast to the future, good fortune and all that, but I know better. A tap on the bar acknowledges the past, those long gone.

Hannah Grace. Imani. Ma. Pa. Even you, Bodachi...you sonofabitch.

A woman in a wide-brimmed hat with predatory eyes floats across the Television in black and white. She's stunning, and I'm not sure if I'm dazed or enraptured, but the barman seems to think so.

He twists to the screen, raises the volume a hair, subtitles in clumsy block text stamp below the film noir. "The Killers," he says, tilting back his fedora. "One of my favorites."

"Seems swell," I say, and sip my whiskey again.

"None of my business," he says, readjusting his hat, rubbing the back of his neck. "But are you alone? Waiting on someone?"

"Yeah," I reply, because it's true on both fronts. I am alone, and I wait on them forever now, for those who aren't coming back. Imani, sitting beside me in that cafe. Me, the cursed nebula swallowing her whole, spitting her out. Hannah, the neglected sister. Me, selfish...all take.

Her blood is a gift, though it always was, and one given for *me*. See, I'm remembering things I was made to consign to oblivion, and in each recollection, she *tells me to forget*. In another motel room. In the back of a rig I don't recognize. Atop a roof overlooking a bay. I must've stumbled on them so many times. She weeps in each remembrance, hates what's happening, all while thinking it's for the best. And can I blame her? If I could only go back, I'd forget it all over again to be with her.

I grip my glass tight as a joyous roar blossoms around me, like nails to a chalkboard.

Be grateful for your sugar-coated lives, because for some of us, waking up we're putting on armor.

The piercing laughter. The clinking glasses. The soda gun firing from behind the bar. The rattle of bottles sliding along the wood. Certain words catch my eye on the Television, and quick as they're there, they're gone. Something about certain women, the chill of a corpse coming off them.

Grief is a hole in your heart forever unsatisfied. Insatiable, and gorging on you a bite at a time.

Hannah sitting across from me in our bedroom. Worry in her eyes.

At that table in that low-lit bar in New Orleans, watching the sheep dance.

Of us sitting atop some rowhouse roof in Baltimore as the city takes on new life across the harbor. My head finding her shoulder, someone to lean on, someone I leaned on for so long without reciprocation.

Grief is a tomb for those left behind. The *true undead.* An impossible weight, and you know? I hope it clings to me forever, because what is grief but unexpressed love? And if I still love her, she's still here somehow.

A scent on the air, and I turn my nose to it. The music dies, and the patrons slow. The same perfume smelled one night near Boston fills the room like an embrace. A quickening heart in a small chest. Boots clicking like the hands of a clock. The door shutting behind her. My heart fills with something I can't explain, something I'd thought lost. The dust blown from what's left of my soul.

I could never remember warmth, not really, but *always* how it made me feel. How I took it for granted.

I exhale, slowly turning in my stool, and she lifts

a hand to me, smiles in her way. As Julia crosses the bar, squeezing between frat boys, dancers, all the others, it takes everything not to squint for her brightness. And I smile, remembering what it is to be warm—know I'm staring at the sun.

ACKNOWLEDGMENTS

So many people to thank, so little space to do so. I want to thank Andrew and everyone at DarkLit Press for their enthusiasm regarding this book and for championing it as hard as they have. I'd recommend those with a homeless story to be mindful of DarkLit's open calls.

To George Cotronis, for the phenomenal cover art. I've worked with George a handful of times, and he always picks up what I'm putting down. Thank you.

To everyone who read this in its developmental stages: J.A.W. McCarthy, Sofia Ajram, Justin Montgomery, Eric Raglin, Micah Castle, and Tyler Henry. Thank you.

Special thanks to Ross Jeffery and Eric Raglin, your nonchalant comments on "Hunger Pangs" persuaded me to follow the thread further. Thanks for reminding me that sometimes, well, a story has legs.

To Charlene Elsby, Cynthia Pelayo, Eric LaRocca, Hailey Piper, J.A.W. McCarthy, and Laurel

Hightower, thank you for taking the time to blurb this novella and for your unbridled enthusiasm. I was humbled by your words and have great respect for each of you.

And to you, reader. Always you. Thanks for giving this story your precious time. Seconds you'll never get back—there's one now...and another. Know that the gift of your time isn't lost on me.

I wrote this for me in one of the darkest times I've ever known, but hope it's for you too.

There is light out there. Remember that.

Scott J. Moses
A café in Rossville, Maryland
November 5, 2022

A NOTE FROM DARKLIT PRESS

All of us at DarkLit Press want to thank you for taking the time to read this book. Words cannot describe how grateful we are knowing that you spent your valuable time and hard-earned money on our publication. We appreciate any and all feedback from readers, good or bad. Reviews are extremely helpful for indie authors and small businesses (like us). We hope you'll take a moment to share your thoughts on Amazon, Goodreads and/or BookBub.

You can also find us on all the major social platforms including Facebook, Instagram, and Twitter. Our horror community newsletter comes jam-packed with giveaways, free or deeply discounted books, deals on apparel, writing opportunities, and insights from genre enthusiasts.

VISIT OUR LITTLE-FREE-LIBRARY OF HORRORS!

ABOUT THE AUTHOR

Scott J. Moses is the author of Non-Practicing Cultist (Demain Publishing). A member of the Horror Writers Association, his work has appeared or is forthcoming in Cosmic Horror Monthly, The NoSleep Podcast, Planet Scumm, and elsewhere. His work has been praised by Laird Barron, Brian Evenson, and others. He also edited What One Wouldn't Do: An Anthology on the Lengths One Might Go To. His debut novella, Our Own Unique Affliction, is slated for release in early 2023 via DarkLit Press. He is Japanese American and lives in Maryland.

You can find him on Twitter/YouTube @scottj_moses or at www.scottjmoses.com.

CONTENT WARNINGS

Alcohol use, suicidal ideation, self-harm, neglect, violence, and musings on the nature of reality How little we know.

DARKLIT
PRESS

CPSIA information can be obtained
at www.ICGtesting.com
Printed in the USA
LVHW041834300323
742969LV00001B/1